LEAH

AMANDA BEDZRAH

EVELYN HOUSE PUBLISHING

LEAH

Unnoticed. Unwanted. Unloved.

Copyright © AMANDA BEDZRAH 2020

All Scripture quotations, unless otherwise indicated, are taken from the Holy Bible, New International Version®, NIV®. Copyright ©1973, 1978, 1984, 2011 by Biblica, Inc.™ Used by permission of Zondervan. All rights reserved worldwide. www.zondervan.com The "NIV" and "New International Version" are trademarks registered in the United States Patent and Trademark Office by Biblica, Inc.™

Editor – Wendy H. Jones

ISBN: 978-1-8383044-0-9

Evelyn House Publishing

Printed in the United Kingdom

All rights reserved. No part of this book may be reproduced in any form or by any electronic or mechanical means, including information storage and retrieval systems, without permission, in writing, from the author and publisher.

This novel is a work of fiction, based on the Bible story in the book of Genesis and should be read as such. There is no intention from the author to suggest this story is historical fact. Readers are encouraged to read the Bible.

This book is dedicated to every woman who has felt rejected. Know that you are completely loved by God and His plan and purpose for your life is not dependant on the acceptance of man.

ACKNOWLEDGMENTS

A book like this cannot be written except by the grace of the Almighty God. Without Him, this book would only be a dream in my heart. I am thankful and truly humbled that God entrusted me with this story, one that had not been written previously; Jesus held my hand every step of the way, whispering thoughts and ideas for this book.

I want to say thank you to my husband Francois and our three children. Your love and understanding enabled me to hide away many days and nights to write. Your support and encouragement was the fuel I needed to keep going. I love you all so much.

I also want to say a huge thank you to my sisters, Efe and Eruke. Your consistent love and support are unrivalled. You girls make life so much easier and you have been with me each step of the way, praying for this book, and listening to all my worries and concerns. Thank you so much.

To my dear girlfriends, you are my biggest cheerleaders. You know that I am so thankful for you all.

To my spiritual mums and mentors – Carol Bostock and

Rev. Victoria Lawrence, your prayers and words of encouragement have carried me through this journey. I am forever thankful.

To my editor, Wendy H. Jones, thank you for helping me bring this book to life.

PART 1

Genesis 29: 1-30

CHAPTER 1

He stirred slightly and panic gripped her, fear seeped out with the sweat from her pores. Afraid and exhausted, she lay awake and trembling beside her new husband. This was supposed to be the happiest day of her life, the day she married the man her heart had yearned for all these years. But the horror of what the morning could bring left her fighting back fresh tears as pain pounded at her temples.

Her eyes, red, and raw were threatening to close tightly from swelling. The pain between her legs from consummating her marriage was nothing compared to the pain within her heart.

Shame washed over her afresh as she recalled Jacob murmuring her sister's name with such passion and tenderness in his voice. His words burned deep within her ears. It felt like with every kiss, every touch, and every thrust he whispered, "Rachel," and yet all she could do was lie on the mat beneath him, covering her face even in the darkness of the night; she endured the pain filled moment.

Now, as he lay asleep next to her, exhausted from the festivities, filled with wine and choice meats and having expended his energy within her, Jacob slept deeply.

She craved for the continuous cover of night, praying that it would remain dark for many more hours. She knew dawn would bring the truth, one she was not ready to face.

A shiver swept through her exposed body and she buried herself closer under the bed covering, wishing it could be her grave instead. The music outside the tent had stopped. Zilpah, her handmaid given as a gift by her father, had closed the tent doors earlier that evening after escorting them into the wedding tent.

Zilpah had sat outside the tent singing loudly as the drummers played to her tune. The music was designed to mask the noise from inside the wedding tent and give the couple privacy. Many hours later, she sat and sang softly long after the drummers had had their fill of wine and lay fast asleep underneath the stars.

Leah looked around the wedding tent which would be their home for the next seven days as was the custom. After that she would be escorted by Jacob to a new tent that he had made specially for her, with room enough for her maid and the children she was sure God would bless them with.

Her tent would be placed near enough to his tent so that she could easily be called to meet his needs as often as he wanted her to. Leah couldn't help but wonder if Jacob would take her to her tent in seven days or reject her presence the very next day.

Although many hours past midnight, it felt like only mere minutes until the first cock crow signalled the breaking of dawn. Leah wasn't surprised to hear the crow; she had been wide awake and petrified.

CHAPTER 2

The last few days played over in her mind until it became a living nightmare. Her father, Laban's voice repeated in her mind as she thought of how he'd told her his plans. *She* would marry Jacob instead of Rachel. He claimed that because she was older, she would marry first.

Leah was shocked; she never expected or even wanted this to happen, but what choice did she have? As a woman she had no voice. To even consider questioning her father's command would be considered unacceptable in her culture. Marriage was discussed amongst men. It was her father's right to choose her husband, or indeed, wager her if he so pleased. Whatever her fate, she had no choice but to agree to his decision for her life. But never once did she think deceit would be a major part of her wedding plans. Something never previously considered had been hatched.

How could a man pay the price for one woman yet receive another? She was the unfortunate plan in her father's devious game. To what end, she wondered.

Eventually, Leah summoned courage and begged her father, trying to reason with him.

She cried.

She prayed.

She begged.

Still, his mind was made up.

She ran to her mother's grave, weeping and praying that this misfortune be taken from her. Her mother, Adinnah, would have known what to do, how to help, how to protect her from this shame and disgrace.

Leah had stopped eating for days before the wedding, a silent protest. When her father was informed, he came to her demanding that she eat and prepare herself for her fate. If not, she would suffer a beating like no other.

His voice, loud enough for all to hear, almost deafened her as well. With nothing more to lose, she wished for death instead. Gathering every ounce of her courage, she spoke up and said, "No, Papa, I cannot do this thing you command." Defying him to his face terrified her demonstrating the strength of her feeling.

Fresh tears fell down her already wet face. She lifted a trembling hand and dashed them away.

She remembered how her father stopped, turned to look her straight in the eyes, and simply asked, "Do you have no love for this man, Leah?"

Her unexpected silence gave him pause. When no sound came from her mouth, he turned and walked away, sealing her fate.

All this while, she thought she had hidden her love and desire for Jacob so well. How did her father know? Who else knew her dirty secret? Who else knew that she had longed for the man who was betrothed to her sister?

CHAPTER 3

Despite previous efforts to stop crying, tears still poured down Leah's face. She wiped them with her now soaked scarf. It was as though the scarf would remove the fresh wave of guilt and shame that tormented her. Through a small crack in the tent roof, the light of dawn peeked in, highlighting the black stains on her scarf from her eye colouring.

Jacob never did see her face yesterday. She wished he had. For once, she looked in the mirror and saw beauty she had not previously seen. Her tender eyes were covered skilfully with black charcoal, and her deep brown hair had been washed in milk and honey for three days giving it a subtle bounce and a sunshine glow. Braided on the top of her head with loose curls falling around the sides and tumbling down towards her shoulders, it was scented with lavender oil. Even now, the soft perfume mocked her. She smelt like Rachel with the wild lavender of the fields that she loved so much. Her father's deception was so calculated and so deep, he made sure every detail was covered down to their very scent.

Leah preferred rose oils because the sweet aroma comforted her. She always dreamed of wearing this perfume as a new bride, yet here she was lying next to her husband, smelling like someone else.

Her lips were painted a deep red, but she refused to stain her cheeks with any colour or wear beads in her hair. She looked just like her mother and she knew it. She saw the look in her father's eyes when he came into the room to ensure she was the one hidden behind the deep blue veil. Raising it carefully as though mindful of her neatly braided hair, he looked at her with a hint of tenderness, "Beautiful," was all he said, and then he covered her face.

Jacob stirred again, wrapped his arms around her and rubbed his palms up and down her back. She could feel the cracks on his palms gently scratching her skin, a subtle reminder of his years of hard work toiling her father's fields and looking after his livestock.

CHAPTER 4

Jacob had worked tirelessly with such commitment and dedication for a little over seven years. His meagre wages, a tent for his head, and food in his belly were not what he had worked so hard for. The real prize lay right here in his arms, his Rachel, the woman of his dreams. So many nights he had lain awake, dreaming of their life together, and their overwhelming love for each other, just like his father and mother's. He had grown up watching their love and desiring a life like theirs: one woman by his side with no concubines.

In time, he prayed that Rachel would bear him sons. He wouldn't mind a daughter, or maybe two, but prayed earnestly to God for many sons.

From the moment he laid his eyes on her all those years ago, even before he knew who she was, his heart was drawn towards her. There was something way beyond her beauty that caught him in its trap. Trying to impress her, he had used all his strength to move the stone from the mouth of the well so she could water her flock. This was a stone that should have been moved by at least three, but love gave him superhuman strength. Oh, did his back suffer for it the next few days, but it was worth the pain to see the look on her face and to put the other young men to shame.

If any man had ever worked so hard for a woman, he hadn't heard of them. These last seven years had been hard, yet it felt like only a few days to him. Is that the power of love he wondered? Now here he was waking up next to her, the woman he had loved and longed for so long. Her scent familiar, as an unmarried man, he shouldn't have known this. However, deeply in love and with a rebellious heart, he had dared on several occasions to get much closer than custom permitted while she watered the livestock.

He wanted to savour their moment of love and make it special and to unwrap her like a precious gift. Had he not drunk too much in celebration the night before, he may have been more patient with her, more tender.

Not quite sure why, he felt ashamed to look at her, disappointed perhaps, at how hard he had dealt with her the night before. How did passion burn within him so greatly that he had no care for this precious woman who was now his wife?

The groom, drunk with wine and passion, makes a bad start to a marriage night. These were the wise words of his father, Isaac, words he now wished he had taken to heart. But he took comfort in knowing that he had the rest of his life to make it up to her. Tonight would be different; they would speak more as they lay together. He would tell her how he had saved himself for her, not indulging in the prostitutes at the pagan temple like many other men. Not even on his father's land had he touched a woman even though he was seduced by Canaanite women many times. His mother had spoken so ill of them for many years, "They are good for nothing but for harlotry," she often said. His brother, Esau's, wife had caused her much sorrow, and he had not wanted to add to her grief by lying with any of those women.

In the company of the men of his youth, he had heard many stories about how to please a woman; he didn't want any practice, and he only wanted her, his Rachel.

Not wanting to wake her up, he turned away from her quietly. He pulled the cover back and rose from the floor on the right side of the mat, stood up, and walked towards the back of the tent where there was a small hole to let in light. He paused briefly to look at her through the pale light of dawn. He saw the red stains on the mat covering, the tell-tale sign of a night consummated with honour.

He stepped out of the tent smiling, happier than he had ever been. A new chapter in his life had begun; soon, he prayed, the sons would come.

Jacob had many thoughts running through his mind as he stood outside the wedding tent and relieved himself. He lifted water from the full pot fetched before sunrise by the maid servant, and washed his face, his hands, and his feet, careful to leave plenty of water for Rachel's cleansing bath. She would need one after the wedding night.

Silence hung in the air that morning, aside from the cries of the various livestock, all else was still. Peace, the sound of peace. Only for a moment. Soon, the wedding feast would continue, and the next seven days would be filled with a celebration of food, music, and laughter by his guests. He and his bride would remain in the tent, enjoying a feast of rich food and wine in addition to the pleasures of marriage. A smile spread across his face. These would be the most exhilarating seven days since his arrival at Paddan Aram.

He approached the inner chamber of the tent with urgency, wanting to catch a brief moment with her, a private moment to express his love again and perhaps hear her say it too. Never once in all the years while they were betrothed did she say it as much as he longed to hear it. Shyness he thought. Even when they spoke, they always made sure they were not alone. There were a few stolen glances and even fewer moments of solitude where he drew near enough to enjoy the scent of the wildflowers that adorned her hair.

CHAPTER 5

Soon after Jacob left the room, Leah knelt down and started to pray. She grew up hearing her mother speak to Abba God and though her father never believed in him or worshipped him, Leah had grown to love her mother's God too. Her mother had first heard of this God from a merchant trader from the Far East. The stories of his mighty works and how he destroyed Sodom and Gomorrah were tales that had been repeated as true for many years to come. No other God had done anything like that before, not even her father's gods to whom he prayed day and night. Did they even hear him?

"Abba, I'm so afraid," she cried out. "Help me. Teach me what to say, give me courage to face him this dawn, I don't know what else to do Abba, please help me," she sobbed collapsing on the floor. Then Leah heard a gentle voice whisper

"Fear not my beloved, fear not."

JACOB HAD ENTERED the wedding tent. Seeing the mat empty, he had called out, "Rachel?". Disappointment washed over him as he gazed around. He had missed her. The servant girls must have risen much earlier than planned to attend to her. Confusion clouded his eyes, until through a mist of pain, he saw her lying on the floor, her head covered. He smiled thinking it was a game and walked towards her. Lifting her tiny frame into his big arms, he swished her around and around, laughing. "You can't hide from me my love," he said as he gently placed her on the soft lamb wool mat that he had specially chosen for her.

Clinging to her head scarf, afraid, feeling dizzy, and nervous, Leah was glad to be lying down again, even though the room continued to spin.

"Are you so shy my love that you deny me the pleasure of your beauty this morning?" Jacob teased, as he lay next to her trying to pull the scarf from her unyielding grip.

Leah lay rigid and wondered why he could not hear her heartbeat. The loud sound deafened her and left her struggling to breathe.

She remembered the still small voice commanding her to *"Fear not."* So why was she still afraid? There was nothing more she could do; there was nowhere to run or hide. All night she had waited for this moment, knowing it would come.

A different type of pain came as the memories flooded in, memories of the tenderness with which he kissed her before he left the chambers, the playful way he twirled her in his arms, the way his voice caressed her sister's name. Jealousy stung, and with it came rage, enough with this 'Rachel, Rachel, Rachel'. She loosened her grip on the scarf and let him remove it from her face and lay there with her eyes closed while angry tears seeped through.

"LEAH!"

His voice shook the tent. A flock of birds, sitting on a tree outside the tent, rose screeching into the sky. She opened her eyes and sat up to face him, filled with inexplicable courage – *"Fear not,"* He had said.

The disgust in Jacob's eyes would be imprinted on her

memory forever "You're unwanted," it said. "You have no place here."

His eyes spoke the message much louder than any words. Not one word was uttered other than her name. Without looking at her again, he rose, opened the tent door and walked away.

CHAPTER 6

*J*acob picked up his outside clothes, walked out of the inner chamber and out the front door of the tent not bothering to greet the servants that loitered outside waiting to serve them, nor did he acknowledge his friends who approached to continue the outdoor festivities.

Anger spurred him, giving wings to his feet as they carried him towards his father-in-law's camp. The gravity of what had been done to him filled him with rage and tears spilled in response to the grumbling of his heart. He walked past the fields; the smell of fresh cattle dung filled the air while hot sand grains filled his unstrapped sandals. He paid them no heed. Walking fast, kicking stones angrily sending them spinning into the distance, it seemed like he wanted to punish the earth for his overwhelming grief. Grief for Rachel.

Leah? It was Leah!

CHAPTER 7

The flap of the inner chamber swung open and Leah's handmaiden, Zilpah, walked in. Without saying a word, she tended to the bed, removed the blood-stained clothes and folded them with care. They would later be placed in the earth, not far from the bridal tent, preserved alongside flower seeds as a testament to her mistress's integrity. She set about her duties to bathe, clean, and prepare the new bride for the second day of celebrations.

Zilpah waited patiently, knowing that in time, Leah would speak with her and she would listen, would console the young bride, and bear her burdens.

When she first heard of the deception, she wept in solitude for the fate of this young girl whom she loved. She had grown up all her life in Laban's household. Her mother had been bought as a slave after they had been abandoned by her father, an Egyptian trader who had defiled her mother with her birth being proof of his crime. Adinnah had taken pity on her mother and bought them as slaves, a kindness they were both grateful for. Slavery in Laban's household was a blessing rather than a curse.

Her mother, Esther, had been Adinnah's friend and companion. The two women had grown close over the years. Her mother had held Adinnah's hands as she wept for many years when another red show brought tears of frustration and pain. Until one month, it seemed like God had remembered her and there was no bleeding.

Her mother had been the midwife when both girls came into the world. Zilpah remembered the day with fondness. She was but a small child herself, sitting outside the birth tent looking through a small gap between the birthing tent cloth. She was charged by her mother to sing sweet songs to ease the pain; Zilpah thought it was more to keep her busy and out of the way.

Leah came out after many hours of pushing and massaging her increasingly frantic mother's stomach. Silence from the baby led to a firm slap on her buttocks and a subsequent loud scream. This made her chuckle loudly, and her mother turned with baby in hand to see her peeping through the hole. Zilpah loved Leah from the first minute she saw her sweet screaming face.

A few minutes later, as the women massaged Adinnah's belly and fed her cooked herbs for strength, she heard her mother gasp and say, "Ah, is that another head I feel? This is not the afterbirth that springs forth." No sooner had she spoken than another baby appeared, and another cry was heard – Rachel, many minutes Leah's junior.

Zilpah was jolted back from that moment at the sound of Leah's heavy sigh. "My lady let me quickly bring you some freshly boiled herbs to soothe you," she said, running outside to kindle a fire and warm root herbs for Leah to drink.

CHAPTER 8

Now the secret was out, the tiredness of a sleepless night overwhelmed Leah as she sat in the basin while Zilpah washed her. She could smell the lamb roasting and knew that the bread would be baked and ready, yet her stomach turned sour within her and no desire for food was to be found.

She knew the meal would have been set in the inner chamber for the bride and groom to eat as one. She would delight in feeding her husband and eating from his own hands too. Once fed and satisfied with wine, the groom would satisfy his body once more.

All seven days of the wedding feast would be filled with food and pleasure while the man prayed that he would be rewarded with an heir.

The wedding date was planned by the bride's servant nurse who knew her ways of the month and what week would be the most fertile. This had not been done for Leah, but for Rachel instead. Her father, clever in his deception, had told few people of his intention; therefore, this week that she married, and she lay with Jacob was Rachel's fertile week not hers.

Leah sighed louder forcing Zilpah to turn around and say, "I have no need to ask what burdens you, as here we are alone with no Jacob waiting to receive you."

Fresh tears fell down Leah's face; she cleaned them wondering if they would ever stop. She was filled with shame. The only thing she dared to ask her father for, that he willingly gave to her, was Zilpah. For this, she was very grateful to him.

She had no doubt that Jacob had gone to confront her father. Her head throbbed at what might transpire between them. Jacob would not dare strike her father, would he? Although old, her father was strong and possessed finely honed knife skills. Now she wondered if her husband would return safely. Gasping for air, she didn't even realise she had stopped breathing; Leah stood up and stepped out of the basin.

"Dress me. Hurry. I must go to my father's house," she said.

"No, my lady," said Zilpah, more firmly than she should have dared. Bowing her head and softening her voice with respect, "Please don't go. It is against our custom for you to return to your father's house." Pausing to give time for reason to sink in and seeing her mistress's resolve weaken, she decided not to push further. "Let me finish preparing the meal, and you can rest. You need all your energy for the week ahead."

Leah could not deny the wisdom of her maid's words. "Rest? I don't need to rest. I shall join you to cook and await my husband." Leah could not believe the words she had just spoken. "My husband."

Never in the seven years that she longed for him did she ever believe she would utter those words. It had only been a few short weeks ago her father told her of his plans.

"Your eyes betray you, my lady, they tell a story of a sleepless night," whispered Zilpah. "If you will allow me, I will cover them with some black kohl and stain your cheeks with colours of red berries, but you must rest a while; even a little sleep will give you some strength."

They retreated to another chamber in the large wedding

tent. Zilpah dressed her in a fine silk garment. A long red dress with gold stitches flowed freely around her, tucked only around her waist. Jacob himself had chosen the fabrics; he had bought them as one of the many preparation gifts for his bride to be. He had chosen carefully and had chosen well. The soft fabric soothed her skin. Her tiny frame was hidden beneath it. Lost in her own thoughts, Leah wondered what Jacob would say when he saw her dressed in a garment he meant for another? Her sister? More tears flowed as though from an endless river within her soul

"Rest nothing can be changed now," said Zilpah, as her eyes wander to the stained cloth she removed earlier to be buried. She bent down to carry them away.

Earlier, Zilpah had returned to the chamber to place fresh linen on the mat. In only a matter of moments, Leah was fast asleep.

CHAPTER 9

The long walk to Laban's camp felt much further than Jacob remembered. He had purposefully pitched his tent far away from his father-in-law to establish his own camp somewhere with no possibility of interference. His need for haste today made him regret that decision.

Filled with burning anger, he picked up his feet and ran, the sound of his sandals slapping on packed earth, muffled by the hot air. His father-in-law's camp, one of the largest in Haram, shimmered in the distance. Sweat trickled unnoticed down his face.

In the seven years he had worked for Laban, his uncle had prospered considerably, giving him pitiful wages for his effort. His main prize was to be the woman he loved as his wife. Jacob had saved his wages, buying livestock for himself, as well as gifts of fabric and jewellery for his wife to be.

He had watched his uncle squander his wealth on temple prostitutes and wine and had watched his cousin's steal from their father's flock for nothing more than merriment with their friends, for their father's blood ran in their veins. These men revelled in women, wine, and worshipping false gods with their bodies and sacrifices.

Jacob hurried, tripped on a loose rock and stumbled forward, narrowly missing a huge tree stump. That did not stop his body meeting the ground. He now bled from cuts on his hands and knees. Ignoring the blood and pain, he kept on walking and running in equal measure, not even a painful ankle stopping him to tend to his injuries.

"How dare he? How dare Laban do this to me?"

He spat the words out into empty air as the sound of his sandals hitting the ground kept time with the furious beating of his heart.

Jacob only felt the pain in his leg when he stopped in front of Laban's camp. Ignoring it, he stood outside and screamed at the top of his voice, "LABANNNNN. LABANNNN."

A small crowd began to gather and people stared. They pointed and started to whisper.

"A new groom in his father-in-law's camp?"

"It's a bad omen."

"He's outside the marriage tent. What kind of marriage is this?

Filthy and bloody, Jacob didn't care. His voice grew louder, "Laban, I demand you come here now."

Laban's household slaves began to gather and whisper outside their feeding tent where they usually gathered at sundown.

"What would make a new groom so angry?" one said.

"Was there no honour on the cloth?" another whispered, and in less than a few seconds the news had spread among the servants that the bed was not stained.

CHAPTER 10

In moments, the tent latch was raised and Laban commanded Jacob to come inside.

Jacob, tears streaming down his face, was exhausted and in pain. He turned to face his uncle and said, "What is this you have done to me? Did I not serve you all these years for Rachel? For seven years I worked tirelessly for you, toiling the ground day and night while raising your cattle. And this one thing I asked, my reward, my Rachel, you keep away from me? Why? What kind of a man are you to betray me like this? You may worship false gods and find pleasure in prostitutes, but I serve a living God who will surely punish your wickedness."

Laban walked towards the tree stump which served as a table and picked up his hot tea. He had the quiet composure of a man who had just won a battle. He smiled but it did not reach his eyes. His cold eyes show his contempt for his nephew whose appearance was worse than his lowliest slave-- bleeding, dirty, and weeping like a child. Could a woman make a man so weak? Is a woman not only for bearing sons and feeding lust? Yes, he expected Jacob to feel anger at his deception, but not like this. Never had he met a man so eager for a woman as Jacob appeared to be for Rachel. It disgusted him.

Sipping slowly from his cup, knowing his silence provoked Jacob even further, he chose his words carefully. He looked at Jacob again and spoke. "Jacob, how dare you come here looking like this, a night after your wedding? How dare you scream with such disregard for me as your elder?"

Laban walked towards the hole in the tent, which gave him a view of his camp and allowed sunlight to enter. He stopped pacing briefly to look at the crowd outside his tent. Pointing at them he continued to speak, "Look at what you've done. The whole camp stands out there, gossiping, and wondering why a newly married man is in public outside the marriage tent before the marriage week is over. An unstained marriage bed will be their verdict." He barely opened his mouth, yet his voice was clear through clenched teeth. He moved towards Jacob, who retreated, fear moving his feet.

Laban, only a few feet away, glared at him, saying louder now, "If you wanted to humiliate me, you couldn't have done better. Your actions have simply labelled my daughter a harlot."

Wanting to strike Jacob but choosing not to, he stormed away instead.

Laban sat down on a mat and invited Jacob to do the same. Making a scene now would interfere with his plans and could turn the young man's heart hard against him.

"Jacob, before you pray to your living God to ask him to smite me, I ask you - what kind of man leaves his father's house, a man of great wealth, well advanced in age and with poor health?" He stared at the dusty floor before continuing. "Then travels many miles to live and work in a strange land albeit with his mother's brother?" A smile spread across Laban's face as the magnitude of his words dawned on Jacob.

Laban's eyes invited a response knowing there would be none. The young man must know that the tales of his misgivings would have passed on the lips of travellers to his uncle's ears. Watching his nephew's unease, he continued, "Don't you dare speak to me about betrayal, Jacob. If there is punishment for betrayal and your so-called God is a just God, I wonder will he not strike you first?"

Laban laughed as he watched the blood drain out of Jacob's face,

Jacob shifted on the mat. His right ankle throbbed, skin hung loose on his right toe, and there was blood on his hands and knees. Not even the pain or the sight of his bruised skin could erase the shame that washed over him at the truth in his uncle's words.

"Listen to me my boy, Jacob. Unlike you, I am only following our customs." Laban lied, smiled, and anticipated victory. "You see, we cannot give the younger sister in marriage before the older. I had hoped that in the past seven years, Leah would have been married. She had many suitors knock on my tent, but none were able to pay the marriage price. I am a fair man, and I know that you love Rachel. I also love you my nephew, so here is what I propose. Fulfil your wedding week with Leah. Then, I shall give you Rachel as a wife also."

Jacob's eyes lit up and then dulled again as his uncle continued.

"But you must agree to work for me yet another seven years. For they are from the same womb, the wife of my youth who sadly is no more. They are equal in value to me. You cannot serve seven for one and less for the other. Tell me, are you willing to pay the price?"

Jacob sat in silence, contemplating Laban's words. He looked at the much older man who smiled. He knew this had put him in a difficult position. If he chose not to work for Rachel, he would be known as a man who broke his word. A weak man who paid the price for one but settled for another. Also, because he truly loved Rachel, he could not risk losing her, or be alive to witness her married to another. If he refused this proposal, Gideon, who vied for her affections, would waste no time offering his services to Laban.

Another seven years of hard labour? Unfair? Yes. Should he have to pay twice for his bride? Was this a curse of his undying love? But wasn't his Rachel worth it? Who can put a price on the heart's desire? How much does true love cost? The last seven years flew past as he worked day and night. Could he not give another seven years? Did he really have a choice? Was God's hand in this? Jacob pondered his thoughts. His uncle's silence welcome.

Turning his face away from his uncle and closing his eyes, he prayed silently, speaking to a God he had come to know intimately on his journey here seven years previously. This was the same God who had given him wisdom and through the years and helped him prosper in this land.

His uncle was correct. What right did he have to speak of betrayal? Jacob prayed earnestly.

"Don't Serve."

The words came as a command that seemed to echo from his soul. At first Jacob was confused. How could God ask him to walk away and refuse his uncle's request? He loved Rachel; he wanted her for himself. No, it couldn't be God that spoke, maybe what he heard was fear.

CHAPTER 11

Laban watched the young man wrestle with his dilemma. It was a shrewd move on his part, a real gamble, one he hoped would pay off. Since Jacob arrived, his business had flourished. The young man had worked tirelessly, and Laban's wealth grew. Jacob's God had helped him and the people of the land to prosper. He would gather regularly at the gate to eat and do business with the other men of the town. The townsmen all agreed that Jacob brought them all prosperity. Another seven years of servitude and this prosperity would flourish further.

But it wasn't just his need for a hard worker that had motivated his deception. He was not entirely a hard man, or so he thought. Laban loved both his daughters. Each was unique in her own way. They were similar in appearance and stature yet opposite in personalities. Leah was more like her mother; her outward appearance could be regarded by many as dull and unattractive. She was happiest cooking, cleaning, or weaving baskets for sale at the market. Her weak eyes and pale skin didn't detract from her beauty, merely hid it. Like a treasure waiting to be found, Leah's true beauty was in her heart: soft, tender, honest, and true.

Rachel, on the other hand, was lovely to behold. She loved the outdoors, running around with the flock all day, and walking for hours to feed them. This left her skin golden and her form beautiful. Laban thought her beauty a special gift from the gods.

From the moment she was born, her smile stole hearts, and she grew more beautiful with every passing year. There was only one other woman whose beauty she could rival - her Aunty Rebecca. Laban could see why Jacob loved her, most men did. Yet, her beauty was used to hide her carefree tongue and sometimes cold heart.

Men were often unwilling to wait and look beyond a woman's beauty and into her character. When he decided to marry his wife, Adinnah, many men had laughed at him and asked why her? Of all the beautiful women, he chose her. After many years of peace, love, and a good life he never once regretted his choice. His only regret was not being able to afford all that was required to appease the gods who ultimately took her life. She was snatched from him by a mystery sickness a few short months after the girls had entered womanhood.

Since she died, Laban had worked tirelessly to grow enough wealth, build his flock and sacrificed more to the gods he worshipped.

He watched his nephew wrestle with his choice. He waited patiently and allowed his mind to wander back to the first day Jacob arrived – one he would never forget. Rachel had been so eager to take the cattle to the well to be watered. She enjoyed her job as a shepherdess, but, more so, she loved the attention she got from the young shepherd boys who worshipped her. Laban had heard from one of his house servants that she had her eyes set on one particular boy, leaving him frightened for her honour. He had decided to find her a husband quickly. When he heard Rachel run into the house in excitement shouting, "Papa. Papa," nothing had prepared him for coming face to face with his nephew. What a joy it was. Handsome and strong, Jacob was a welcome sight to behold. It was many years since his sister Rebecca left, chosen as a bride for his cousin, Isaac, who dwelt in Canaan. She went there with her nurse, Deborah, and he had not seen her since, but he had heard that she had prospered, bore two sons, and fared well. It was a pleasure to meet his nephew and hear all about his younger sister and her family.

After the initial pleasantries, as custom dictated, they sat to enjoy a meal of freshly baked bread and a year-old lamb that Leah had cooked for the men of the camp. As she served them, Laban watched in surprise at the besotted look on Leah's face. One look at Jacob and her love for him was both obvious and sealed. For the first time, he had seen a spark in Leah's eyes as she opened them in wonder at the first sight of this man.

Over the years he watched Leah look at Jacob with fondness when she thought no one was watching. Perhaps no one else was, but he knew his daughter and loved this girl whose smile had been hidden until Jacob came. Jacob brought out the smile that lit his daughter's pale face. Laban knew that Jacob had never once noticed Leah beyond a, "Thank you," when she presented him with a meal. He had not once bothered to look up.

Leah enjoyed household duties, so her father put her in charge of the camp.

It was Leah's job to ensure that the men and the household were fed. She was not required to serve them personally, yet each day she chose to serve her father and Jacob, even if Jacob did not notice her.

CHAPTER 12

"Yes, I will serve another seven years," Jacob's sober voice echoed in the almost empty room interrupting Laban's thoughts. Aside from a few rugs, and a wooden stool, the large room outside Laban's private tent was bare. It was not a place for entertaining but a good place to talk about things in private. Laban looked at Jacob, unsurprised at the answer. He knew Jacob would do it. Only for a brief moment had he doubted because of Jacob's extended silence.

Jacob got up to leave. He turned and said to his uncle, "I will quench the rumours; your daughter is not a harlot." He couldn't even bear to say Leah's name.

Disappointment washed over him. He was still filled with a rage he could not express as he battled inner demons over what had been done to him. Did everyone know the scale of the deception heaped upon him?

Laban stretched his hand out and Jacob took it. The deal was sealed. Another seven years of work had now commenced. He looked at his nephew, taking in his injuries. "What happened to you, Jacob? How did you hurt yourself so?" Laban pointed at Jacob's rapidly swelling toe.

"I tripped as I ran here blinded by rage."

"And now? Does rage still fill your bones?"

Jacob raised his head to respond, without lifting his eyes. "No rage, only disappointment and shame."

"You need a nurse and an escort home," muttered Laban.

"I will be fine. I've suffered worse. I will see myself back to my tent." As his mouth snapped shut, he turned and walked away.

Laban escorted his nephew the short distance towards the tent door. "Jacob, you are a good man, and I love you as a son. It is because of this I say to you, don't lose sight of what you've got because you're blinded by what you want. Leah is a good woman, a good wife. Even though you feel betrayed and you long for the one you don't yet have, you already have something wonderful: a good woman. It is not for me to tell you how to run your household, yet I beseech you to honour her, respect her, and make the wedding week all it should be." With that, he bid his nephew goodbye, watching him as he weaved his way through the rapidly dispersing crowd. He saw Jacob pause periodically to quench the rumours he unwittingly started earlier.

CHAPTER 13

Rachel had heard Jacob's screams as they shattered the otherwise silent air. She remembered when she first heard she had been betrothed to him. At first, she thought him old and unsuitable; she was keen to be with Gideon. When her father informed her that she had been given as a promise to Jacob, she knew her future was mapped out for her. So, she set her heart on Jacob. Over the years, she grew fonder of the older man and appreciated him. She enjoyed the way he stared at her in awe and the times he dared to come close enough to drink in the smell of her hair.

She'd spent the last seven years dreaming of what her life would be like married to such a man and giving birth to his many sons. She came to love Jacob as she listened to her friends talk about how handsome he was and how lucky she was to be loved by him. It was their jealousy of his love for her that made her desire him more.

As her wedding day approached, Rachel was ready. She had learnt all she needed from the older maidens about how to satisfy a man's stomach as well as his loins. The date had been carefully chosen to coincide with the week of her fertility. This was carefully worked out by her nurse according to the days of the moon. Rachel felt ready. The crowning glory of every woman was motherhood. A few of her childhood friends already had sons suckling at their breasts and told tales of the pleasure of motherhood. She could not wait for her own moment, for her own tent, and to be the woman of her own household.

A few days before the wedding, her father revealed to them a new plan. The brides would be swapped on the night of the wedding. The deceit was so great it placed a heavy burden on her heart. A wicked game was being played and Rachel could do nothing but weep and pray as their father had forbidden her or Leah to speak to anyone, especially Jacob. Their disobedience would bring disgrace to his household.

Neither of them was given a choice. She watched in shock and sadness as their futures were decided at their father's words. Leah cried tears of anguish. Rachel wondered if the despair truly reached her soul or if it was laced with unspoken joy. Bitterness towards her sister boiled in her heart for the first time as she remembered that day.

Their differences in personalities had never been an issue and their relationship was strong. A deep bond bound them, a love that blossomed year after year. They were friends, they were sisters, they laughed, they played, and they spoke about everything. So many nights, Rachel had told Leah all her dreams and hopes for her future with Jacob. Yet here they stood in front of their father and Leah was willing to take her future husband at papa's command.

Quiet resentment built within Rachel and she looked at her sister with contempt.

When Laban left them alone, Rachel turned to Leah, "Why would you agree to marry him? This is what you have wanted all along, isn't it?" she spat out, her voice laced with venom.

Leah's tears flowed freely as she spoke, "What would you

have me do? Say no to Papa? Have you not heard me try to disagree? Do you think this is what I desire?" She quickly realised reasoning with her sister was futile.

"Why are you not willing to die instead of doing this wickedness to me," Rachel replied through clenched teeth.

Leah rose from where she had been kneeling to beg her father. She looked at Rachel and whispered, "I have no hand in this deceit. You know I have no choice but to obey Papa. If you wish me dead, then kill me yourself." She turned and walked out of the tent, without looking back.

CHAPTER 14

It seemed like a long night as Rachel wrestled with her memories as well as thoughts of what the morning might bring. What if he chose Leah? Would she now be shamed? Everyone knew that she had been betrothed to Jacob. All her friends and all the slaves. Everyone. Oh, how she would die of shame if she was not redeemed from it by Jacob. Could a man really love that much? Work another seven years? Despair set in as she waited for what would happen after the wedding week passed.

The first sure sign of hope was seeing him at her father's camp that morning. His anger clear to all. She never expected to see him that day. She had thought the wedding week would be long gone before Jacob would approach her father to question the deception. How could the groom leave the wedding tent? Had he killed Leah? Terrifying thoughts crowded her head, and she rubbed her temples.

She had been afraid that Leah would please him so much, he wouldn't care about the deceit. She tossed and turned all night wondering if her sister would take her place for good. The thought made her frantic. For seven years, she had waited to be married to Jacob.

At first when her father betrothed her, she was furious. Jacob was much older and not as exciting as the young shepherd boys. But as the years went by, she came to terms with the idea of her betrothal to Jacob and looked forward to not just being a bride but bearing many sons. Love would come. Her best friend Mara had told her so.

Mara had been married to a man her father's age as his third wife. At first, she detested her husband, but after she suckled two boys and a girl she spoke of her marriage with such joy. She had found peace and love in the arms of her children and had grown to love her husband. Recounting the stories of her friend's marital passion excited Rachel. She wanted to be a wife and also experience the joy of consummation and motherhood. Love would come. She was willing to wait.

Rachel knew how much Jacob loved her; he had never stopped saying so. Seeing his rage that morning was proof, even though she didn't need it.

If all was well, she wouldn't care if Leah married him first. "Stupid tradition," she whispered. Never once had she heard it spoken of. Mara even said so herself; she too was married long before her older sister.

Yet, Rachel could not argue with Papa. She knew all he wanted was Jacob's labour to bring him greater prosperity. This was not about tradition or custom, this deceit was about her father's greed. But what if her father's plan hadn't worked? What if Jacob said no and rejected both women and returned to the land of his father. Who could blame him? What man would work fourteen years for one woman? Never before had this happened.

The night before the wedding, Rachel was tempted to go and tell Jacob the truth. She was unable to rest, worried that he would not work another seven years and she would miss out on the joy of being his wife and all that entailed. Covering herself with a large scarf, she left her tent, hurried past the back exit and out into the front yard. The sleeping sun hid her.

How would she tell him? What would she say? Not pausing to think, Rachel quickened her step.

"Rachel." Simon's voice beckoned her. How stupid of her not to realise that her father's man slaves would be out in the courtyard.

"Should the bride to be be walking in the shadows of night or resting for the week to come?"

Without responding, she walked back into the house feeling defeated. She had no choice but to wait.

Now, as she watched Jacob walk away, her heart pounded with desire. She pulled of her scarf and discarded it, not caring about the fine fabric. She stamped her foot and said, "Why did Leah have to get there first? He was mine."

Her father hearing of her evening wandering ordered her to be consigned her to her tent until she was summoned. With a slave outside her tent and no other contact but for food and water and not even from her usual maid servants, Rachel sat alone with her thoughts and her fears. Waited - thinking, life could be so unfair.

CHAPTER 15

Jacob started his journey back to the wedding tent, annoyed with himself that he refused the offer of an escort. A donkey or camel ride would have done his leg some good and eased his throbbing head. Now he was tired, in pain, and hungry. He knew there would be a freshly made meal waiting for him, but he was in no hurry to face Leah. He chose instead to sit under a fig tree.

Plucking its ripe fruit to eat, he gathered his thoughts as he ate. The juice from the fruit ran down his cheeks as he ate with reckless abandon. For the first time in many years his past came back to haunt him. He remembered what brought him here to this land all those years ago.

CHAPTER 16

*J*acob was the younger twin born to Isaac and Rebecca. His mother often told the story of how he was born clutching his brother's heel. There was an unspoken rivalry between the boys. Both were skilful in their own ways: Jacob with livestock and Esau with wild game. Esau, the first son was much loved by his father and Jacob much loved by his mother. In return, he loved to be by her side where he learned to cook, sew and farm.

As the boys grew, they learnt to worship their father's God and offer sacrifices to him from the work of their hands. One day, Jacob had cooked his mother's favourite meal. He saw his brother Esau approaching, hungry and tired. Seeing the stew in Jacob's hands, he begged him to give it to him. Jacob, a swindler and true to his name, sensed an opportunity and bartered with his brother - his birthright for a plate of stew. Esau, despising his birthright willingly exchanged it for a bowl of lentil stew.

Taking the left-over stew to his mother, Jacob couldn't wait to share the good news. "I've bought it Mama. It's mine; it's mine; it's mineeee." He danced with joy before presenting the stew to his mother, Rebecca, spilling some of its contents.

"Oh Jacob, would you waste my favourite meal with your joy?" she said as she tried to scoop the stew back into the bowl. "What has you so worked up? First come and hug me and let me kiss your cheeks for I love them so." She playfully reached out to her son as he entered into her warm embrace.

"Esau came to me hungry, and I asked him for his birthright in exchange for some stew. He said it's of no use to him if he's dead with hunger. He even swore an oath, so I am now the first son."

Rebecca smiled at her son as she remembered the words from God about the two nations fighting within her womb, and His promise that the younger would be greater than the older.

All these years nothing had come of that promise. Esau had walked around like a king, supported in his superiority by his father Isaac. Rebecca loved both her sons as a mother should, yet her heart was always with Jacob and his heart with her.

"Son, the birthright is not enough," she said. "It doesn't mean anything without the blessing. As well as Esau's birthright, you will also need your father's blessing."

Sensing the change in Jacob's mood, she sought to reassure him. Putting down her spoon, she took her son's hand and looked into his eyes. "For as long as these breasts have fed you and these hands have raised you, and I still have life in my body, I promise you Jacob you will get your father's blessing as the first-born son."

Although comforted, Jacob's eyes displayed uncertainty. "But how will this happen? Papa is not going to honour the exchange between Esau and me. You know he won't. He's always loved Esau more than me."

Rising to her feet to get some water to drink, Rebecca laughed loudly "Ah, Jacob, of course he is not just going to give it to you, you're going to have to take it. When the time is right, I will tell you what to do. Don't worry." She picked up her spoon and dug it into the stew. "Come now, let's share our meal.

You've learnt well my son. You can rival me with your cooking," she teased him, and they both laughed.

With the afternoon sun now beginning to shine brightly, Jacob plucked another fig from the tree and moved further onto the side of the road. He sought shelter underneath some large oak trees. Wiping sweat from his forehead, he looked down at his toe and knee, both of which looked in urgent need of a clean cloth and some herbs. He knew it would sting but it would stop infection and ease the pain that was sure to come later. Mustering up his courage, he continued the trek home despite the pain.

Not too far from the tent, he stopped to rest again, careful to avoid a place that would draw attention from a passer-by or worse, a friend. Being a shepherd meant he was well versed on the whereabouts of hidden paths, and over the years he had come to know this land intimately. He sat upon some soft grass putting his now swollen leg on a stone to rest and allowed his mind to wander back home again to his mother, remembering her with fondness. With an ache in his heart he whispered, "Oh, Mother, if you were here today, you would know what to do. You would know how to advise me." He breathed in deeply trying to remember her face and the warmth of her embrace.

CHAPTER 17

The opportunity for the blessing didn't come for many years after Esau exchanged his birthright. Over the years, he had tried many times to buy it back. Once, he cried bitter, frustrated tears while accusing Jacob of being a thief and stealing his birthright. Jacob replied by calling his brother stupid and lazy. Chastising him for being a fool to be blinded by his love for food, he pointed at his brother's protruding stomach and said, "Look, there's your birthright in your huge stomach." This fight was harsher than all the others.

Their mother, as always taking Jacob's side, banished Esau to sleep outdoors with the wild beasts. She claimed that as he behaved like one, he could sleep like one.

AT THAT TIME, their father, Isaac, was old and losing his sight and his mind. A few weeks later, Rebecca overheard Isaac calling Esau into his tent. He asked Esau to make him a fine meal of wild game after which he would bless him. This was the moment she had been waiting for. She called Jacob and told him of her plan. Now was the time to steal his brother's blessing. She immediately sent Jacob to bring game from their flock for her to cook. Using the animal's fur, she made hairy hands for Jacob. She then ordered him to dress in his brother's clothes and sent him to his father with the meal she had prepared. Isaac recognised Jacob's voice. However, because the meal was cooked to his liking, the hands that delivered it covered in hair, and the smell of his son familiar, he blessed the boy richly.

When Esau arrived and found out what Jacob had done, he was filled with overwhelming rage. He swore an oath to kill Jacob.

Rebecca was afraid for her son's life. She knew what Esau was capable of doing, He was a skilled hunter and bigger and faster than his brother. She had heard the rumours of Esau plotting to kill Jacob and knew that she needed to protect her beloved son. So, she visited Isaac, her husband, pleading with him to send Jacob away, back to her homeland to choose himself a wife from among her people. She complained that Esau's Canaanite wives were a burden to her, and she did not want to have to deal with any more troublesome women.

Isaac agreed, which is why Jacob ended up serving his uncle for the bride of his dreams as his wage.

REMEMBERING his own wickedness from his past, Jacob was filled with regret. Is this what betrayal felt like? It was painful to walk in his brother's shoes. Jacob sat under the tree turned towards heaven and cried, "Can I hide away from my own wickedness, my God? Can distance erase sin? Have I not first wronged you? Another seven years is not enough to repay my own errors for I too am a man who has run from his own deceit." And with that, he wept bitter tears and slept.

CHAPTER 18

❦

*L*eah looked out from the tent wondering where Jacob was or if he would return. The morning meal had grown cold and the afternoon feast was now starting to endure the same fate. She refused to eat the meal that had been set out for two. Although feeling much better after a few hours sleep, she paced around the inner chamber. "Abba, where is he? Please keep him safe," she prayed.

Another hour passed with Leah now certain Jacob would not return to her. She began to pack her things. She knew the shame of a bride returning only one day after the wedding night would be unbearable; she would be destined to die alone and never remarry as she would be considered without honour. She wouldn't even share the pity given to a widow; her shame would be much worse, a discarded woman destined to become a slave in her father's house, relying on the generosity of others to survive. No son. No husband. No honour.

Overwhelmed, she decided to run to the other side of the river. "Oh God," she prayed. "Please forgive me. Take me home to you; this is all too much for me to bear."

She put on her sandals and left as quietly as she could to

ensure no one saw or heard her. She planned to escape through the side of the inner chamber. Kneeling down at the far corner, where the earth was still soft, she lifted the hard wood that held the thickly woven goat hair in place. It was well made and firm, so Leah heaved at it, trying not to make a sound. The wood did not move, and Leah sighed in defeat. Perhaps she would simply cover her head and go out through the side entrance, as though she was going to relieve herself.

She successfully stepped out unnoticed and moved quickly through the small camp into the quiet of the forest, as she walked purposefully away from the camp. A gentle breeze brought with it a familiar voice with a message of hope, *"Go back home my beloved, trust in your God."*

Leah stopped stock still.

She knew the voice of her Abba; she had heard Him speak to her ever since she was a little girl. But knowing His voice and hearing His command brought dread instead of the usual comfort. Go back? He wanted her to go back? Back to what? Back to whom? Didn't even her Abba want her? After she had served Him all these years and refused to bow even to her father's idols, she chose instead this unseen God. And now, she was willing to offer herself to Him as a sacrifice and He didn't want her.

"Go back," He said.

Leah turned around to trudge the short journey back home.

CHAPTER 19

Jacob was startled awake. Instantly alert, he thought, 'what was that sound?' He was not sure how long he had been asleep, but he knew he must head back into the camp before night fell. He had to face Leah. What would he say to her? Should she be punished for her father's decision?

His mind wandered back to Rachel and a deep longing for her overshadowed his reasoning. "Six more days," he whispered. "I can wait six more days." He walked back to his camp, his steps slow, and approached the wedding tent. The pain in his heart mirrored the physical pain he felt. His leg, now visibly swollen was a constant reminder of his foolishness. He saw a small gathering of people, eating and drinking outside the tent, and squinted his eyes to try and make out who they were. Was Leah out celebrating with them, he wondered?

Choosing not to be part of the celebration, he moved swiftly to the side of the tent. Hidden by his cloak, he entered the tent without being seen. The guests outside were now sated with wine and roast lamb with only the bones left and the bread baskets almost empty. They probably wouldn't have noticed him even if he walked right through the middle of them.

Jacob walked into the wedding chamber and saw Leah on her knees praying. She turned and screamed at the sight of him and rushed to his side taking in his wounds. "Oh, my Lord. What has befallen you?" Tears streamed down her face, and she fell to her knees at the sight of her husband. She stepped out of the tent and only a few minutes later returned with clean cloths and herbs and tended personally to his wounds.

Jacob was surprised at how gentle and tender she was as she attended to him. It would not have been unheard of for her to call her maid to serve him instead. She carefully undressed him and tended to his wounds. She prayed as she used a wet cloth to clean him from head to foot.

Jacob relaxed at her touch and allowed her to care for him. A mixture of guilt and pity squeezed his heart causing it to miss a beat. Clearing away the dirty cloths, Leah stepped out of the chamber and left Jacob alone with his thoughts. She returned with a variety of fruits, bread, meats, and wine and fed him. Jacob ate out of her hands as he rested his weary head on the side wall of the tent. He gazed at Leah. For the first time since he arrived in her father's camp many years ago, he saw her as the woman she really was – tender. After a bellyful of food and wine, Jacob drew her close.

CHAPTER 20

Over the next few days, Leah felt joy like she'd never previously experienced. Her husband had accepted her. She chose to tend to him personally, cooking for him, feeding him and laying with him as often as he wanted. Jacob seemed to relish not just in her exquisite cooking but also in her equally exquisite body and the woman he now realised she was. Her heart was content.

Zilpah was vexed at all the work her mistress chose to do.

"Let me do my job and serve you both this wedding week, Mistress. You do your job and stay indoors with your husband."

Indignant, Leah had insisted her job was to cook, clean, and feed her husband and the sons to come, so she wanted to do so right from the very beginning.

Zilpah had laughed at her, teasing her about being so besotted, but Leah didn't care. Zilpah was right. She was unashamedly in love with her husband and grateful to God that he had returned to her and had loved her so tenderly these last few days.

She didn't bother to ask him where he went that morning and why he returned so late and in such a state. He was lord over her, and his presence was enough for her. She decided in her heart to do everything she could to make the rest of his days filled with joy and his house filled with sons and daughters. She would build his camp exceedingly.

Joy filled her heart. Tonight being their last night together, she prepared to make it special. Tomorrow she would be escorted to her own tent that he had made especially for her. A sudden frown crawled across her face at the realisation that the tent had been built for Rachel, not her. Would he escort her there tomorrow? Thoughts buzzed around in her brain. Tomorrow would usher in another phase of her married life, one where she was now free to visit her family and friends. Would Rachel be more welcoming to her? How would she treat her? She missed her sister and prayed that this marriage wouldn't be a thorn that would tear them apart. Rachel could so easily be betrothed to someone else she thought. Her beauty was rumoured throughout the land. She could even be married to a foreigner, one of great wealth. Their father could have received so much more than seven years of labour for a beauty like hers.

The past few days with Jacob had been filled with simple talk of food and procreation. Tonight, Leah wanted to have a proper conversation with him and get to know her husband more intimately. It would be their last night where she could be in his presence without being invited. Once she was escorted into her tent, she would have to wait for Jacob to either come into her tent or she was summoned to his. How often would this be? She wondered. Tonight would be a good time to ask him. Tonight, she would ask about his hopes and dreams, and how many sons they would pray to come along. Tonight, she would ask about his childhood and anything else he would be willing to discuss. She would listen with wonder and make every second count. If she could keep him awake long after the lamp burned out, whispering in the dark, she would. Tonight, would be special.

CHAPTER 21

*J*acob tossed and turned on the empty mat. Leah had left him to cook and prepare herself for their last night together. He wondered why she insisted on doing these things herself when she had a maid servant and his own male servants to help. Yet, it was admirable that she insisted on this and he admired the zeal with which she gave herself to him, holding nothing back. Jacob wondered if Leah was simply obedient to her father or if she had secretly loved him all these years.

If the latter was the case, she had never once shown any signs of it or he had simply never noticed. She was a good woman; she was kind and respectful, but his heart longed for Rachel. "One more night." He smiled. He had done as Laban had asked him to; he had been respectful and treated Leah as the wife his custom demanded of him. Tomorrow, he would escort her to her tent. Jacob's eyes darkened as a frown knit his brow... which tent? Definitely not the one he had lovingly built for Rachel. This one was positioned only a few steps away from his own. No, that tent would be Rachel's. He would have to escort to a different tent on the far side of the camp. The visiting shepherd's tent would suffice. That would ensure enough distance between the sisters.

He allowed his mind to wander back to Rachel. Their night tomorrow would be so special, with no need for a big celebration. The wedding rites would be swift, his reward handed over to him, and another week of festivities would begin. Jacob decided not to drink too much wine this time. He would savour every single moment of the coming week, and maybe he might even keep her in his tent for many weeks afterwards. "My Rachel," he whispered into the cool evening air.

CHAPTER 22

*L*eah walked into the chamber with her clothes loosely draped around her. She carried a jug of wine in her left hand and a plate of warm bread, fish, fresh pomegranates, and dried dates in her right. Already she knew his favourite meal and placed it in front of him just how he liked it. She smiled sweetly as he motioned for her to sit beside him.

"My husband, tonight I want to feed you and please you even more than I did these last few days. Will you show me what to do?"

Jacob looked at her and smiled, one of the joys of any man was a humble and willing wife. In Leah, he had both. She prayed to the God of his fathers and chose not to worship any idols, which surprised him. From the first evening when he had returned from his uncle's camp until this very moment when he watched her kneel before him, Leah had prayed. She prayed like a woman who loved God with every fibre of her being.

"You already please me, Leah. My week has been filled with good food and the pleasures of you and your body."

He picked up a slice of bread, dipped it in olive oil, and bit into it. Oil trickled down his beard, and she wiped it way. They sat quietly and enjoyed the meal together. Jacob picked up a cup of wine and held it to her lips to allow her to drink.

Leah delighted with his affection, drank deeply, much more than she had ever done before. The wine rushed to her brain and loosened her tongue. "I am glad my husband has forgiven the deception of my father and received me. I was afraid of your rejection and had reconciled myself to a life much less than that of a widow. But here I sit at your feet as you serve me from your cup. I pray that God blesses us with many sons and fills this camp with the sound of children. I pray too that my beloved sister Rachel will be blessed with a husband who's cup she will drink from too."

Jacob choked and spilled the wine over the mat.

"My husband," Leah screamed, rushing to soothe him. She removed the scarf from her head and placed it on the mat to soak up the wine.

At that point Jacob realised she had no idea what was to come. "Leah…" he stuttered. The rest of the words stuck in his throat.

Jacob had imagined that her father had shared all his plans with both sisters. Now, he realised the extent of Laban's wickedness.

"Yes?" Kneeling at his feet again, she said, "Is all well my husband? I beg your forgiveness for mentioning Rachel."

Jacob looked at Leah and the look on her face pierced his heart. She was merely a woman and he a man with rights to do as he pleased. Why then was he afraid to tell her the truth of her father's plan?

"Tomorrow, I will be taking Rachel as my wife; I will work another seven years for your father. I will escort you to the tent on the other side of the camp while I start my wedding week with Rachel. Once it is complete, I will work with the male servants to build you another tent on the far side of Rachel's."

Leah could see his mouth move, she could actually hear what

he said, but her brain refused to accept the words. Her world collapsed around her. She held back the tears, refusing to allow him to see her weakness.

She would not cry.

She would not be subject to his pity.

The rejection stung deep as the realisation of what he had just said began to sink in. Rachel was coming tomorrow, and she would be an outcast on the other side of the camp.

Earlier in the day, Zilpah had started to move Leah's things to the newly built tent. It was furnished with oak and timber, and the cooking area was well stocked with foreign herbs and spices. The mat was carefully woven with soft linen made from lamb wool. Zilpah had told her everything about the tent and how wonderful it was, a home for a princess. She could not step inside the tent until the wedding week was over, but she already knew it intimately, through the eyes of her maid servant. She knew where the sleeping mat was, she knew where the daytime areas were, she even knew the corners of the tent that would be expanded for the children as they came along. Just beside the tent was the room for Zilpah and beyond that was where the other servants stayed.

While the wedding tent was beautiful and indeed filled with everything that was needed to make the week memorable, Leah was ready to move into the place she could call home. One where she would raise her sons and welcome her husband for many years to come. And with her husband's words, that dream was swept from under her feet. It felt like there was no more air to breathe. Holding back tears and holding her breath was a terrible combination for in a few seconds, she was face down on the floor.

"Leah," Jacob screamed, rousing her after a few seconds that felt like a lifetime. Jacob carried her and laid her on the mat. He saw the tears she tried so desperately to hide behind her wine-soaked scarf. The one she used to clean the floor when he spilled his drink earlier.

Searching for the right words to say but finding none, Jacob tried to console her. It would have been much kinder of Laban to have told her the truth the minute the plan was hatched.

Guilt whispered his cowardice to him. Laban alone should not bear the responsibility. Besides, how would Laban have known he would agree to work another seven years? It was his duty to have informed Leah that he would be taking her sister as his wife also, a duty he should have performed days ago. Not knowing what to say, he set the food aside and lay with her. She received him but even he could tell her body responded out of duty; the warmth and comfort that has pleased him these last few days seems to have faded.

CHAPTER 23

Leah wept quietly even as Jacob fell asleep beside her. She replayed Jacob's words in her mind. They sounded like a dirge with no need for music or no actual death. Her heart mourned. How could she be sharing a husband with her twin sister?

Fresh tears fell freely, as easily as they did on their wedding night. "My God, my Abba, why is this happening? Should I be like one who is like a widow, yet my husband is still alive?" Leah knew that Rachel would scorn her for the rest of her life. Rachel would receive the new tent, the one lovingly made by Jacob himself. She felt cast aside like a used wash rag by being sent to the old tent at the back of the camp.

How would she tell Zilpah that she needed to remove her belongings from the superior tent? Oh, the shame. It was common practice for a man to have many wives, to bear him many sons to build his camp, and make his name great. Leah had been ready for that. She had thought that in a few years she would willingly give her maid Zilpah to her husband as a concubine. Perhaps in her older years, finding a few others to bring into their household. It was done by many; it was expected; it was acceptable; it was the joy of every household to have a camp overrun by women and children. But never had she heard of a man taking sisters as his wives. Not once. How then could this be her fate?

"Abba, why didn't you let me die? I cannot bear this pain. I cannot lift my head up from this shame. Oh Father, I cannot enter into a battle with my sister I have no hope of winning. Jacob's heart is with her. Who holds mine?"

"I do."

A voice as clear and real as if it had been spoken aloud rather than whispered in her soul came again.

"*I do my beloved. I hold your heart.*"

And with it came comfort and rest. Leah closed her eyes and welcomed a peaceful sleep.

CHAPTER 24

The morning of the eighth day dawned. The skies were grey with low hanging clouds and the scent of rain. The rising sun was hidden by a dark cloud, giving the day a menacing feel.

Rising early Zilpah prepared for the day ahead. Looking up at the sky, she wondered which god was angry. This looked like a day where sacrifices would need to be made. She resigned herself to the tasks of the morning and planned to take out her carved idol much later in the day to pay homage and offer sacrifices. The idol had been a gift from her mother a few days ago. Bidding her farewell, she handed it over as her protection for the new life ahead of her.

Today, she would move into the back room of Leah's new tent. There, she would look after her mistress, waiting on her every need. Leah needed complete rest to ensure maximum fertility for conception. Leah had insisted she wait on her husband, for the wedding week which had been chosen was Rachel's fertile week and not hers. Laban could not risk asking for Leah's week to be the wedding week as his plans would have been exposed.

Zilpah, recognising the truth of her words, had agreed to step aside and give Leah the pleasure of serving her husband. She knew Leah was grateful that Jacob had returned to her, even after such a momentous deception. She had watched Leah worry and listened to her cry into the afternoon following the wedding night. When Jacob did not return for many hours, she tried everything she could think of to appease her mistress. She sang songs and told tales from years long gone. Nothing seemed to dry her eyes until his return.

Her thoughts were interrupted when Leah walked into the bathing tent.

"Ah my mistress, you are up earlier than I expected. I will draw water for you and clean you. Then I will wash your hair with the oils you love the most so the fragrance will fill your new tent." Zilpah winked at her.

"It's not my tent. It's Rachel's. She arrives for her wedding week today."

The bucket clattered to the floor and a pool of water gathered around Leah's feet. Zilpah stared, frozen, mouth open, unable to speak or move. This was unheard of. Marrying two sisters! Zilpah looked upon her mistress with compassion. Jacob must have informed her the previous night. What a coward, she thought. This whole week Leah had loved him beyond what any other wife would. She was so grateful to have him that she had worked hard to win his love. Was all of that effort for nothing? When Rachel arrived today, what would happen to Leah? Tears welled up, but she needed to be strong for her mistress. She recognised the tell-tale signs of a sleepless night, and it was not from enjoying the marital bed. Without thinking, she moved over to Leah and drew her into a warm embrace. They collapsed on the floor weeping tears of both bitterness and loss.

CHAPTER 25

Jacob was awakened by the sound of weeping. He rose and drew closer to the noise. He heard two voices whispering. He recognised Leah's voice but couldn't make out what she said. He knew that voice intimately - the softness of it when she spoke his name. The other voice was her maid, Zilpah. He thought he knew what was being said and was grateful he couldn't hear the words because they would no doubt be unpleasant.

The joy of today was somewhat overtaken by the sorrow from the night before. Why did he wait so long to tell her? He turned around in the room and saw the half empty jug of wine from the night before. He picked it up and drank long and hard, ignoring the cup nearby. The morning was wet and windy, and he could smell the grass from the fields almost as powerfully as he could hear the sound of the raindrops. He walked back to the mat and lay down. He needed to rest for the day ahead. It would soon be time for both sorrow and joy. He would take Leah out and welcome Rachel in.

CHAPTER 26

*L*eah was packed and ready by the time Jacob rose again for their last wedding meal. Most of the guests had left the previous night. This morning, only a few should have lingered to form part of the escort party to her tent. Jacob looked around and saw that they had also gone. Perhaps Zilpah had bid them all farewell.

Only a few morsels passed Leah's lips as they sat quietly eating their last meal together. Her warm smile had gone and was replaced by quiet obedience. She didn't stop responding to him, but her tenderness had been replaced by fear. It seemed like she lacked the courage of the last few days to pick up his meal and feed him. Jacob missed that. He missed her soft fingers carefully touching his lips and lingering even after he had taken the food. He looked at her, longing for her to feed him, even just one last time. She lowered her eyes from his and he realised it wasn't courage that she lacked, but confidence. He had stripped it of her. Only seven days after her wedding and another woman was taking her place. Whose heart was more wicked he wondered: her father who caused this confusion or he who accepted it? He felt like both victim and accuser in a wicked game. One where everyone but Laban got hurt.

If he had chosen to wait one year to marry Rachel, which was usual for taking a second wife, would it have been fair to make her wait? Even after only seven days with Leah, his heart was moved with compassion towards her. What would a year of her gentleness have done for a man like him? Would it not have killed his love for Rachel? Jacob looked at Leah and again hardened his heart. She didn't have what it would take to steal his heart from Rachel; he could not be held responsible for their father's deceit.

If any curse was to be on anyone's head, it would be Laban's. He, himself, had dealt kindly with Leah when he could have rejected her. She should be grateful he didn't. He would escort her to the other side of the camp and then hasten to Laban's camp to fetch his new bride. A rush of excitement filled him and set his loins on fire, dampening his guilt. He could lie to his heart and maybe even his loins, but deep down, in his soul, he knew that something in him continued to long for Leah. She was the real victim in this nasty game, and he pitied her. Maybe that was what he truly felt, he thought: pity.

CHAPTER 27

Laban gathered some of the men together, his sons, and four of his closest friends.

"Jacob will soon arrive, but until he does, let the feasting and drinking begin."

They laughed, cheered, and made merry. Laban could not describe his happiness at his good fortune. Another seven years of Jacob working for him would bring him great prosperity. It was evident that Jacob's powerful God was with him, for Jacob's hands were blessed and so were his field and livestock. Since his nephew arrived, his flock had doubled and thrived. Jacob had done more than all of his sons combined. Seven more years was all he needed, and he would be an extremely wealthy man. All it cost him was his daughters. At first, he had hesitated at the idea of marrying off his daughters to the same man.

He looked at his friend, Rotheus, as he drank cup after cup of wine. Laban smiled to see his friend rejoicing with him and coming to terms with his plans. Raising his own cup, he drank deeply and was thankful. Weeks ago, when he had shared his plans with Rotheus, he had initially quarreled with him.

"Why would you set up your own daughters against each other?" he had screamed. "Jacob loves *Rachel*. What life would you bring upon Leah? Would you sow seeds of enmity between them?" he asked, shaking his head.

"What has love got to do with bearing sons and raising a household, Rotheus? Tell me, was the fourth bride who was dragged with tears in her eyes to your household filled with love for you?" Laban paused, then continued before his friend could answer. "My daughters will have honour in their husband's house, and I will profit greatly from it. Should that not be the matter we discuss? Their union will earn me fourteen years of income and my household will increase."

Rotheus looked at him and said, "Yes, yet my four wives have aged me greatly. Over the years, love has come and for this, they are at war with each other over my affections." He gazed at the ground and then lifted his head to look Laban straight in the eye. "But I tell you the truth my friend, the war amongst women who are strangers will not run as deep as the war amongst sisters. You have set up Jacob to be the first and last to marry sisters. There are other ways to acquire great riches, my dear friend. Think carefully about what you are doing."

With that, he took up his sandals from the ground, dusted them off, and left.

The sound of loud laughter brought Laban back to this day, this moment. Recalling Rotheus's words he wondered if he should stop this wedding. Could he not just offer Jacob a fair wage, a portion of the land, or come to some agreement to make him stay longer instead. But what if Jacob was displeased and rejected Leah? Jacob would be within his rights to recover the profits from the last seven years of work. Everyone knew the truth that there is no such custom to marry the first daughter off first and if the matter was brought before the elders at the gates, shame would fall upon his household.

"No. This wedding must go on," and with that, Laban rejoined the crowd of men, eating and drinking as they awaited the new groom.

CHAPTER 28

Rachel awoke with mixed emotions that morning. It had been seven long days since her older sister was married to the man meant for her. The one for whom she'd waited for seven long years. Today, Jacob would return and take her as his bride, the one he loved.

She had been locked up by her father for the last seven days with an unfamiliar maid as her attendant; therefore, she knew nothing of what had been happening in Jacob's camp.

She had no way of knowing if Leah had been accepted and loved by Jacob. She wondered if Leah would be in the tent that Jacob had made for her. Over the years, she had seen the dedication with which Jacob had cared not just for her father's flock, but for his camp, his servants, and his tents. Tales had been told of him weaving by hand, mats, coats, and bed coverings from the softest of goats' hair. He had chosen to decorate the bride's tent himself and had even chosen all her gifts, fabrics, and jewellery individually. It had made him a laughingstock in front of the men as rarely did any man go to such lengths for a woman. Rachel had revelled in being the object of such intense affection. Now, the sting of shame and embarrassment was one she couldn't seem to shake off. What would people say? After everything she had said, after all the ways she had taunted the other girls. The ways she had made jest of those who had married as second or third brides. She remembered with regret how once, angry at her sister for not helping her with her own chores, she had revelled in taunting her with her predicament. She reminded Leah that no one had ever asked for her hand in marriage and laughed bitterly while she said it, delighted that it made Leah so unhappy. She had watched Leah run into their late mother's empty tent and do what Leah did best, cry and pray.

She had also unintentionally brought her dear friend Mara to tears. Mara had come to share her news of being married off to the much older Ham, a skilled musician and wine merchant. He already had other wives and many sons. Even though it was common practice, Rachel had laughed at the news, telling Mara how glad she was that Jacob would only have her as a wife. She had been quick to remind anyone who forgot that she was worth seven years of income.

She knew she was the envy of many. Both her beauty and her husband to be were desired by others. She loved to hear the tales of Jacob's exploits at the merchant site or how hard he worked building the wedding tent and her own tent.

Never did she imagine that Leah would take her place. Never did she imagine that she would have to share her husband.

Opportunities to talk alone were few and far between. Jacob made the most of them, keen to express his commitment to her. Only a few weeks before their wedding, he had sent her a message of his love along with a bunch of cut flowers larger than anyone had previously seen.

A deliberate mixture of smells and colours had both excited and intoxicated her. She turned around to look at the now dead blooms discarded in a pile at the corner by the door. She sighed.

She desperately wanted to pray; these last seven days she had prayed to the Lord of her mother only once. Then she turned to the gods of her father, clutching tightly to the little idol she was able to procure from Daniel, the man servant her father had ordered to guard her.

She knew many of the girls and women of Paddan Aram would be gossiping about her at the wedding feast; at the well, in the market, near the fields, as they washed dirty garments, or even as they cooked meals. Everywhere they gathered. They would rejoice at her ill luck, happy that she would now be one of them. A second bride. Tears spilled down her already wet cheeks. How could such disgrace befall her?

Bilhah walked into the tent and saw Rachel crying. She simply whispered, "My mistress," she bowed her head in greeting. Unsure if they were tears of joy or sadness, she busied herself with laying out the garments for the wedding and preparing the accessories she would use to enhance her mistress's already beautiful face. Earlier that morning, she had been summoned by Laban and informed that she would not only lead in preparing Rachel for her wedding but, in addition, would serve as her handmaiden going forward.

She had been quick to pack her few belongings, ready to move to Jacob's camp with Rachel. Serving her would be no easy task, as her new mistress could be caring or wild, depending on her mood. She had seen Rachel tenderly care for a baby goat when it was born deformed; she had also seen Rachel smack a young servant girl harshly across the cheek for disobedience. Bilhah had everything prepared and was ready to dress her mistress. She escorted Rachel to the outhouse where she spent time washing out the milk and honey that was put in her hair the previous night before being wrapped in palm leaves. Rachel's hair was thick, curly, and midnight black and hung all the way down below her waist.

Rachel broke the silence, "Don't braid my hair. I will wear it loose today," she said more firmly than she intended. "Have you heard anything said about me?"

Bilhah let go of Rachel's hair and started the mud scrub. "No, my mistress, I have kept busy in the food quarters, cooking, and cleaning. There have been many guests from Moab coming with cattle to trade"

Rachel was relieved, perhaps there was no idle gossip after all. She had hoped her friends would be at her wedding feast, but her father had sent word that her wedding would be a brief exchange in his tent with only a few witnesses. There would be no big celebration. Just enough food, music, and wine to fill the belly of his own friends and their camp. There would be no escort party to her tent and no seven days of food and music afterwards. It had all been done already for her sister who had already had the wedding meant for herself.

Fresh anger filled her, how could the man who bore her be so cruel. Her father had stolen so much from her, and her sister had enjoyed everything that she should have had herself. She was denied the first rights to her husband and also the right to a wedding feast in her honour.

Bilhah looked at her mistress with pity. Sensing her fear and anxiety, she went to pick some root herbs. On her return, she soaked them in hot water and wine to help her mistress relax. Despair was a look that could not easily be hidden; it clung tightly to Rachel's eyes, deepening their colour and hardening her face. The circumstances surrounding the wedding were not favourable and she had lied when she said nothing was being said at the well. This was not the day to recount tales, there would be plenty of time for that. She prayed to the Lord to give her wisdom and teach her what to say. Watching her drink deeply, she started to put flowers in her mistress's hair and then painted her face. Even after hours of crying, Rachel looked beautiful. No paint was needed to darken her eyes or stain her lips; she had a natural beauty that was lost behind any colours.

They hid the sun's glow on her skin, the freckles it left spread across her dimpled cheeks. Her nose looked too small for her face, but only because her lips were full and well rounded.

Bilhah had skilfully covered her eyes with kohl and stained her cheeks with red berries. Her maid picked up the red paint for her lips, but Rachel pushed her hand away. "No. Leah's lips were red. Find me a different lip paint. Purple, brown, any colour but red."

"You are so beautiful my lady, and it is *you* Jacob loves." Bilhah started to sing quietly.

When Rachel saw her wedding clothes, she was pleasantly surprised. The colours were rich and vibrant. "Who chose this? It's gorgeous," she said, displaying the first hint of excitement all morning.

"Your father sent it with me; he instructed it to be kept aside for you. It was among the fabrics Jacob bought." A huge smile spread across her face.

Rachel stepped into the garment and for the first time felt like a bride. Her dress was designed to cling to her body, and her face would not be covered at Jacob's request. Even though her father had no other daughters, Jacob had insisted that she didn't wear a veil.

All her fear and anxiety started to fade away. Maybe it was the wine, or the beautiful dress, or more than likely, the quiet reminder of the truth – Jacob loved her!

She started to sing along with Bilhah, ready and waiting to be summoned by her father to marry the man who loved her.

CHAPTER 29

⌘

For the second time in a short span, Jacob was dressed in wedding clothes. He planned to walk alone to Laban's house to marry his bride. Everything had happened so quickly, leaving him no time to plan for another wedding. His few friends had to return to their own lives the night before and his male servants had been sent to the fields to tend to the livestock and farmland.

He allowed his mind to wander back to dawn; Leah had awakened and was praying to the Lord Almighty. He had never seen a woman so desperate to know about God. She had enjoyed listening to him teach her everything he knew about God and also the stories he heard from his father Isaac. He remembered the look on her face when he told her how God had tested his grandfather, Abraham, asking him to sacrifice his only son Isaac. She had jumped with joy, spilling wine over him when he told her about the miracle lamb that was provided in Isaac's place by God. She loved the Lord and everything about Him. Her tearful prayers were quiet, even in joy she cried out to the Lord, speaking from her very soul. This was a tender and intimate relationship. He remembered longing to be worshipped by her the way she worshipped her God. This was a love like no other.

Leah had walked quietly to her tent with him beside her. An awkward silence lingered between them, as neither could muster up any words. He was a man with rights to more than one wife, he thought, and concubines could also be chosen, so the feelings of a woman should not hold any weight. Yet, guilt hung over him as he left her in her tent and walked away. That was a few hours ago. It was now well past midday, almost the hour for him to undertake the journey to Laban's camp. The memories of her eyes still lingered. It was the look in her eyes which had him so confused.

"Lord, you know my heart and love for Rachel, please make this burden light," he whispers to God. Quiet desperation swept over him, bringing a melancholy that any man should not feel on his wedding day. A knock on the door startled him, he stepped outside to see a small gathering of men led by Zilpah and two other female servants from a neighbouring camp accompanied them.

Zilpah had baskets of food and jugs of wine to hand. He turned and saw some of the women from the other side of the village approach his camp as well, one of whom he recognised having seen her with Rachel on many occasions. They were all dressed in wedding clothes. Confused, Jacob summoned Zilpah to his side. "What is going on? Why are all these people here?" he asked her. A frown narrowed his eyes.

"At well past dusk, my mistress asked me to gather the best of what was left of the wedding feast and prepare all I could lay my hands on. She also instructed me to go before dawn and hire escorts and knock on the doors of Rachel's friends and find all willing to come to be part of the wedding feast."

"Leah did this for me?" He asked, surprise shining from his wide eyes.

Not sure if it was a question or an observation, Zilpah nodded her head and walked back to the small gathering.

Jacob welcomed the entourage and together, they headed to Laban's camp.

Leah looked from behind her closed tent door; she watched the small crowd as her eyes fixed on Jacob. She heard his laughter and took in the way he tossed his head back. She watched as he moved ahead of the crowd with only a slight limp from his newly healed foot. As he walked away, her heart broke with every step he took.

Leah looked up to heaven and to God and asked, "What will my future be, Lord? My husband and my own sister? Wouldn't death have been kinder?" she cried.

Aware that she was alone in the camp, except for a few slaves on the other side of the fields, she tore her clothes in mourning and let out a loud scream. And then she heard His still small voice speak:

"Trust in me. I am the Lord who loves you."

CHAPTER 30

Laban watched the small crowd approach and immediately recognised the groom. They were all singing and dancing. At first, he was both annoyed and surprised to see the crowd. Where did Jacob find these people to escort him and who was supposed to feed them? There was barely enough wine left as they'd started the festivities early, unsure of what time Jacob would arrive. As they came closer, he saw the jugs of wine on the women's heads and the baskets of food they carried. A smile started, at first only a hint then spreading across his face. It would be a proper feast after all.

"They are here!" Bilhah screamed in her excitement. Rachel jumped up and peeked through the tent door. Her heart filled with joy. She saw Mara and Sarah dancing too, and on seeing Zilpah, she wondered why she was here instead of at Leah's side. Beaming, she turned to Bilhah. "Quick, put on more kohl and purple lip stain on my lips."

Bilhah opened her mouth to tell her mistress that her face didn't need more colour but fear meant she did as requested.

Following Jacob's arrival, she waited much longer than she

expected for her father to appear outside her tent. He entered, looked at her, and smiled. This was the first time he had seen his daughter since the night before Leah's wedding when she was caught trying to escape to Jacob's tent. Her betrayal could have cost him so much; he would have been obligated to stone her to death for her disobedience. "You look as beautiful as always," was all he said before he covered her face with her veil and led her to his tent.

Jacob stood up as they approached. Laban had kept him and his guests engaged in mindless chatter, eating and drinking their fill of the wine and food they had brought. Jacob had avoided too much wine; after his last wedding night, he had vowed to be drunk only in the comfort of his own tent. A flash of anger swept over his face as his veiled bride was ushered in. He had specifically asked for her not to be covered.

She stood in the middle with her father, waiting to be welcomed to his side for the marriage rites to be said and their hands to be joined. As she stepped closer, Jacob looked at Laban and said, "Unveil the bride that I may look upon her face as I speak my rites to her." A quiet murmur filled the room as they turned and looked to see what Laban would do.

Laban had not expected to be publicly challenged by his nephew, even though he had every right to do so after what had already happened. Despite this, he could not shake the anger he felt towards Jacob. Regaining his composure, he smiled. "Of course. Yes, of course."

Laban motioned Jacob forward and invited him to unveil the bride. There would be other ways to put this little boy in his place. Let him have his moment today.

Jacob walked towards Rachel; his footsteps were unsure in his nervousness. Although only a few steps, it felt like a vast journey. The seven years he had worked and waited to marry Rachel had flown by more quickly than those few steps. Taking a deep breath, he felt the almost palpable silence from the crowd as they waited for the veil to be removed. Jacob prayed while he lifted the edges of the veil. He knew Laban would not be so stupid as to trick him a second time, but he also hadn't expected Laban to trick him the first time.

He took another step closer and knew immediately it was her. He didn't need to remove the veil; she smelled of wildflowers and the fields.

He lifted her veil, saw her, and in an instant, caught a glimpse of his mother, Rebecca. His heart was filled with even more love. His mind connected with his heart as buried memories flooded in. She reminded him of the first woman to ever hold his heart; she was the image of his mother - her aunty.

She smiled and her tongue rested in a way that teased him. She lowered her eyes as his pupils widened. She was beautiful.

His Rachel!

Lost in her, he didn't even hear the crowd cheer.

He was brought back to the moment when his father-in-law slapped him on the back. "Let the rites commence," said Laban. The music, cheering, and laughter filled the tent and echoed around the camp. The discarded veil lay on the floor and his bride kneeled by his side. The rituals began and were complete in only moments. They were married. He was ready to head into the wedding tent with his wife.

They sat together as man and wife while they were served with choice meats and wine. The servant girls left shortly after to prepare her bags, and soon the escorts were ready. They would sing and dance all the way to Jacob's camp. The bride would ride on a donkey pulled by her groom.

Jacob arose in a hurry to leave. A week earlier, he had been too consumed with wine to care after having planned such an elaborate ceremony. The food had been plentiful, and the wine had flowed. Not this time.

He knew the wedding tent would be clean as Zilpah had seen to this the minute he moved Leah to her own tent.

Saying his final goodbyes and glad to be taking his wife home, Jacob and his crowd left Laban's camp. There was rejoicing as they walked back to Jacob's camp.

CHAPTER 31

Rachel looked down from the donkey that carried her and stared at Jacob who was pulling the reigns. She smiled. There was a crowd around her with music and dancing. It was well past dusk and so the oil lamps were used for light, softening the darkness that surrounded them.

The music was soothing even though loud, and it made her smile from the depths of her soul. She had had a feast; she had a crowd; she had a wedding celebration; she had her friends come and witness Jacob profess his love to her. There was no one who didn't see that look, the one where his mouth hung open and left him needing to wipe it with his cloth. And now, she was heading home to their wedding tent, a tent he had shared with her sister these past seven days.

Her stomach churned at the thought and inwardly she vowed that she would do everything she could to make sure Jacob never called for Leah again. She had his love and after tonight, she would have his body too. She would captivate him and please his manhood with everything she had learnt from Mara's older sister, a temple prostitute. Once she was settled in her new home, she would go to the temple and learn some more. Leah would never lay hands on Jacob again. Never! She laughed, the sound echoing into the cool night.

Home was in sight; her future awaited. She would be a mother of sons and daughters safe in the arms of the man who loved her. As they approached the camp, Jacob saw the oil lamps had been lit in the tents and his household was still awake. The servants from the field came out of their tents to welcome them home. Leah's tent was hidden behind the others, so he couldn't see if she stood outside or not.

There was cheering and the music grew louder as Rachel dismounted from the donkey into Jacob's waiting arms. He carried her into the wedding tent, and as he approached the door, the familiar smell of lentil stew filled his nostrils. The porridge, one of his favourite meals, sat on a tray of leaves with freshly baked bread, fish, pomegranates, figs, a jug of fresh water, and a jug of wine.

Although it was barely furnished the room had an unexplained warmth and it was arranged differently. There were freshly cut flowers strewn around and stalks of lavender lay around the mat on the floor. Jacob also noticed the hay underneath the mat had been refilled. Leah did this. In his haste, he had left no instructions to his few servants, so Leah had ensured her sister was given a feast and escorted and welcomed to her new home.

A surprising warmth filled his heart and he decided there and then he would call for her after he'd spent seven days with Rachel. He would call for his first wife and enjoy a few nights with her.

He walked over and laid Rachel tenderly down on the mat. Jacob looked at her and smiled. He watched her reach for the food laid out for them; she must be hungry. She hardly ate anything during the wedding feast and neither did he. Rachel dished a plate for him and set it before him. She then dished another plate for herself.

Jacob took his plate and sat beside her waiting for her to share her meal with him, to feed him out of her hands. She smiled at him as she lifted a tiny morsel of bread, dipped it into the stew, and put the food in her own mouth. And then again, she broke the bread and continued to feed herself.

Not able to shake off his disappointment, he looked at the food set before him and began to feed himself. He reached for the jug of wine and didn't bother to pour it into a cup, drinking long and deep from the jug. He left only a few drops behind. They both ate in silence for the next few minutes while exchanging love struck glances.

Bilhah was welcomed in to remove the empty cups, dishes, and the empty jug of wine. She left behind the water and carefully closed the door behind her. Only a few minutes later, she was sitting outside the playing the drum loudly while she sang. The sound was intended to masquerade the cry that would erupt with the breaking of her womanhood.

What a joyous day it had been, a day that had started with tears was ending with joy. The wedding, though much smaller than most, had been a success. Her mistress was happy; she was happy, and she thanked the Lord Almighty while she sang the songs of her ancestors. She sang songs of praise and prayers for sons and daughters.

Jacob took Rachel and laid her carefully on the fresh white cloth that had been expertly placed on the mat, waiting to bear the signs of the integrity of their consummation. After seven long years and what seemed like seven longer days, here she was in his arms, the woman he loved, the woman he would have to work another seven years to earn. He pulled her close and knew her intimately. Through the night she wanted more of him, and she beckoned him onto her. Had the oil lights not gone out many hours earlier, and had he not endured the resistance that came with the breaking of the bond, he would have lifted the cloth to see if there was a stain with his very own eyes. She moved about him swiftly, knowing what to do and where to touch him. She pleased him all night and long into the morning.

For many days, Jacob and Rachel were locked in their wedding tent, their mouths speaking little, their bodies speaking much. Jacob was delighted in the arms of his wife and didn't realise nine days had passed and they were still in the marriage tent.

CHAPTER 32

*I*t had been nine days since Rachel arrived and Leah had only seen Rachel from a distance. She was waiting until her sister was in her own tent so she could talk with her about ways they could live in peace. They had been close friends growing up and talked about everything. Rachel was put in charge of their father's small flock of sheep while her brothers tended to the larger livestock. She enjoyed the outdoors and the company of the other shepherds. Sometimes she was gone for many hours in the day, finding green pastures for the flock to feed on, or waiting at the well for the stone to be rolled so the animals could drink. There were times when she would go with her father and brothers to other towns to buy or sell livestock, and once, she went with them to shear the lambs and was gone for days.

The distance between them was subtle at first. Her younger sister used to look up to her and listen to her. But when their mother died, it was up to Leah to look after the camp and be the woman in the home. Her father had concubines; they often came and went from his tent and eventually one bore him more sons. Still the responsibility fell on her as the first daughter in the home.

She relished in taking charge and enjoyed caring for the household. Her father would often joke that when she was married and gone that his household would fall apart. He would say to anyone who cared to listen that Leah would make a good wife. This sometimes made Rachel angry; she was always quick to remind her father that even shepherdesses could make good wives and that a man liked a woman who was willing to work hard.

Rachel was determined to earn her father's respect and praise and so she spent more time working in the field and less time at home. She spent even less time talking to Leah and instead made other friends. Then when Jacob arrived and she was betrothed to him, she became even more distant and unbearable.

She recalled how only a few years ago Deborah had taught them all the ways of women. She had been their Aunty Rebecca's nurse, and she returned home a few years after Jacob arrived bringing the sad news of his mother's death. She had then stayed with them. That day, she explained the mysteries of childbirth, marriage, and motherhood.

Rachel was sitting next to Leah and whispered, "You don't need to pay attention, no man would want you." She laughed loudly. Leah felt an immediate rush of warmth to her cheeks, the memories as clear as though they happened yesterday.

Zilpah knocked softly on the door of the tent, bringing her back to the present. "Should we serve the evening meal now," she asked.

Leah looked at her, afraid of what the response would be but wanting to know. "Will Jacob and Rachel be joining us?" Her voice barely reached a whisper.

"No, she has not been escorted to her own tent yet. She remains in the marriage tent with Jacob. Bilhah came to take some food to them and complained that her fingers hurt from playing the harp and drum over and over again."

Leah looked up at her unable to hide her tears. "Gather the house and serve them their meal; I am not hungry." She walked to the inner chamber of the small tent, knelt on the mat, and began to weep.

PART 2

Genesis 29: 31-35

Genesis 30: 1-24

CHAPTER 33

"I really need to get back to work; my servants have done well but I must fulfil my duty to your father," Jacob whispered into Rachel's ear. He breathed in the smell of her hair that he had come to love. These last few days together had been wonderful, and he would happily have stayed in her arms for eternity.

She buried closer into him, willing him to stay next to her. She knew that with Jacob going back to work, it would be likely that she would be escorted into her own tent and would have to wait until she was summoned by her husband. Long days in the field could leave a man drained with no appetite for a woman. Also, in the field some distance away he would have time to think about other things, to pray, meditate, and think of Leah. What if he summoned her instead?

Jacob untangled himself, rose, pulled on his inner garments and then reached for his outside clothes. Rachel helped him dress, deliberately touching him in tender places to try and arouse him. He tenderly pushed her away, determined to go back to work.

Rachel's mind raced, thinking of ways to keep Jacob to

herself, thinking of ways to remain in his care for every moment of the day. Then a smile formed at the corner of her lips.

"Rest with me one more day, and tomorrow, I shall go to the field with you. As a shepherdess, I know how to look after livestock and tend the field. We can work together, and I will lighten the burden for you," she said, bowing at his feet and kissing them gently. Jacob put down his cloak and lay with her again. "One more day," he whispered and drew her back to him.

CHAPTER 34

The next day, Leah rose before the sun awakened and headed to the garden. She had fallen in love with this place; the flowers were beautiful and the herbs rich and vibrant. There was a small fig tree she had been speaking to for days as she clipped away its dead branches. This was a place of solace and a place of prayer. When she walked amongst the flowers and trees, she could feel the presence of God. Peace, she felt at peace. Her stomach rumbled loudly reminding her that she had not eaten a proper meal in days. Her heart longed for Jacob and was sore.

It had been ten days since she last spoke to him and had the opportunity to learn more about the Almighty God. Leah enjoyed the warmth of his body but also the stories he shared about their God. He had started to tell her the story of seeing angels climb up and down from heaven, a dream he had many years ago. He had promised to finish telling her the story later. They had prayed together that night and she had heard him speak to God about his desire to have many sons.

Leah rubbed her belly that she hoped would carry his many sons.

"Lord, please let him call for me. How can I give him sons if I do not lie with him at the right time?" she whispered. Just then, she heard a rattle and looked across the camp. Bilhah was taking Rachel's things out of the wedding tent. A smile spread across her face. Would God answer her prayers so quickly? With Rachel moving out, she would now have a chance to see and speak with her husband. She could also reason with her sister and together they could come up with an arrangement to serve their husband well.

Leah stood up, leaving the weeds she was eager to tend and forgetting to pluck the fresh mint leaves to boil for tea. She rushed to clean herself and prepare to visit her sister. She had finally finished the basket she was weaving for Rachel as a wedding gift. It was beautiful; it had her favourite colours, red, purple and green. The basket was filled with soft cloths - remnants from various fabrics. These cloths would be used to wrap the babies bottoms to keep them clean.

Giving her sister a basketful of these items was significant; it meant she prayed for her hands to be filled with many children. That was Jacob's desire too; together they would fill the house of Jacob. She smiled as she folded them neatly. They had been soaked for days and washed in herbs and oils which would soothe any baby's bottom. Leah smiled as she allowed thoughts of the future to flow freely within her. They were thoughts of laughter, love, children, family, food, and feasts.

She walked purposefully with basket in hand towards Rachel's tent. Rachel was facing her direction and she could also see the back of Jacob's head. He was facing Rachel and they appeared to be deep in conversation. After all this time, what did they still have to talk about?

She heard Jacob's deep, booming laughter that seemed to erupt from his very core. How she had missed him and longed to look into his dark brown eyes. The thought of his smile made her tingle inside. She hastened her steps towards them. Rachel's face held no smile or any acknowledgement of her impending presence. Jacob heard footsteps approach and turned in her direction. Rachel pulled him closer to her and urged him to walk away with her.

STANDING in front of the tent, Leah dropped the basket on the ground and sighed. Bilhah came out, saw her, and bowed her head in greeting.

Leah looked at Bilhah and asked, "Where are they going? I thought Rachel would take a day or two to rest in her tent and settle in. I came with gifts and was looking forward to speaking with her."

Bilhah looked at her with discomfort and said, "They have gone to the field together; my mistress insists she will help him tend the flock."

Leah suddenly realised the painful truth; her sister was deliberately going to keep Jacob away from her. She looked at Bilhah and smiled. "Here is a gift for my sister. Please give it to her when she arrives and send word through Zilpah how she receives them. Also, let me know when she arrives and is seated so I can come and visit with her again." She paused for a second to enjoy the scent of the folded cloths before handing the basket to the maid. Then, she turned and walked away.

CHAPTER 35

Jacob walked deeper into the open fields and came to a place of solitude. He left Rachel and the servants to tend the flocks and fields. The last few weeks had left him with little time to come quietly before his God. He sat silently, meditating and praying to the Lord God.

"Leah."

He heard the voice of the Lord whisper her name. Jacob was mildly irritated at the unexpected intrusion of thoughts of her. He started to pray purposefully, giving no more time for the quietness of his soul to hear God speak to him of Leah. He prayed for Rachel instead by blessing her with his words from the depths of his soul. Yet no matter how hard he tried to still the quiet voice, he knew the Lord spoke Leah's name within him. Frustrated, he screamed his defiance out loud, "RACHEL." Picking himself up, he walked back towards the field trying his best to remind himself that Rachel was his choice.

CHAPTER 36

*R*achel sat under a large leafy tree seeking shade away from the hot afternoon sun. Exhausted and wanting rest, she started to regret her decision to come to work. Her place was now at home not in the field.

Her mind wandered back to seeing Leah carrying the basket towards her tent that morning. She wasn't sure what Leah wanted, but she was sure she had no interest in finding out. She laughed to herself again, remembering the way she diverted Jacob's attention from her sister. It was so easy; Jacob hadn't even noticed Leah. She knew that she would have to speak with her sister eventually and knew she would not bother to hide her intentions from her.

"You're not having him, Leah," Rachel said with confidence, even when the only audience was the swaying leaves above.

She determined in her heart that Leah would be Jacob's wife in name only. Leah had obeyed their father in this deception, and she had had her seven days and would have no more.

CHAPTER 37

※

Leah lay quietly on the damp grass in the garden she had come to love. Only a few feet away from her tent; this somewhat hidden patch of wildflowers had become her place of solitude. This was a place where she cried her heart to God in peace and escape from the attentions of her maid. Zilpah's insistence that she saw a nurse was becoming tiresome. Yes, she had lost much weight and her clothes needed extra stitches at the sides to hold them in place. But who could blame her? Her life was worse than a widow's plight.

Her husband treated her no better than a servant in his household, without warmth, without the familiarity they had shared for those seven days. She had not had one quiet or even intimate moment with Jacob in over three months.

A few weeks ago she had summoned up the courage to go to Jacob's tent since he chose not to come to hers. Unfortunately, Rachel saw her walking over and quickly came out of her own tent before walking confidently into Jacob's. When Leah finally arrived, Rachel rudely informed her that Jacob was fast asleep and could not be disturbed. Not wanting to cause a scene, Leah had simply walked away listening to the sound of her sister's laughter.

After that, Leah stopped trying. Messages sent through Zilpah came back with empty promises of a visit soon but that visit never came. Not once did Jacob knock on her tent door.

"Lord won't you look down on me with mercy? Have you forsaken me too? My heart is filled with sadness. My story is told with pity. Even my handmaidens and the household servants have more joy than I." Fresh tears fell down her face as she continued to pray silently. Suddenly, her stomach turned, and pain gripped her. A wave of dizziness washed through her and she gripped the grass around her in an attempt to steady herself.

A few moments later, she rose and returned to her tent calling out for Zilpah to attend to her. "Please, fetch me some mint tea. My stomach has turned on me."

Sitting down on the small wooden stool made out of an old tree stump, Leah leaned her head on the wall beside her.

A few moments later, Zilpah returned with the hot tea and a portion of fish and bread. Leah pushed it away; the smell of the fish was inexplicably repugnant to her. She loved fish; it was her favourite thing to eat, more so than lamb or goat. She knew that was why Zilpah brought it to her.

"You need to eat, Leah. Please. Not eating won't make Jacob….." She stopped mid-sentence remembering her place.

"Won't make Jacob what?" Leah snapped. "Go on say it. Won't make Jacob what? Love me?" Shame and anger washed over her. She had become an object of pity. She had heard the gossip and seen them whisper and stare as she walked past. It was bad enough that she was relegated to the far side of the camp, but so much worse that only Rachel was ever seen stepping in and out of Jacob's tent.

Even when they all sat down for the evening meal together, Jacob sat beside Rachel. They spoke, they laughed, they ate like one family, but she was never alone with Jacob. Everyone saw her plight; everyone saw her shame.

The rumble in her stomach brought her back to the moment as she rushed out of the tent and emptied her stomach of what little food remained. Shortly after, she blacked out and Zilpah screamed.

CHAPTER 38

Deborah placed a cool cloth on Leah's head. The young woman looked malnourished, weak, and tired. Deborah had been praying when Zilpah burst into her tent screaming that her mistress had fallen. The men were out in the field and Laban had been gone for many days to buy more livestock and grain. She was glad Laban wasn't there to see or hear of his daughter's predicament. Although a shrewd and wicked man, he loved his daughter and would have been furious to see her in such a state. The words she had heard whispered among the servants were true. Jacob had failed in his duty to look after his first wife because he focussed solely on Rachel.

"Poor child. May the grace of the Lord be upon your head and upon this child within you," she whispered, as she removed the cloth to dip in the cool water ready to place on Leah's head.

Although Leah was very thin, the small bump rising in her stomach was unmistakeable. She was with child and she probably didn't even know it.

Zilpah came in with food - fresh baked bread, some fruits, a jug of watered wine, and roast lamb. She placed them beside Leah.

"When was the last time Jacob called for Leah?" asked Deborah.

"Not since the wedding week," Zilpah replied solemnly, shaking her head.

Deborah looked at Leah who was now fast asleep. "It's been just under four months since the wedding and she hasn't been to him?" She stroked Leah's sweat stroked brow. "Are you sure?" she asked again.

Zilpah nodded her head several times.

"When was the last time the way of women came upon her?"

Zilpah's eyes opened wide in wonder. "Not since we've been here," she said loudly causing Leah to stir.

"Shhhhhhh. Quiet." Deborah scolded her. Waving a hand towards the tent door, she walked towards it.

Zilpah followed, her tread soft.

Once outside, Deborah said, "It would appear she is with child. The Lord has looked down and seen her sorrow and blessed her with this child" She looked towards the tent door. "Watch her while I go back to Laban's camp and pull a few things together. I will stay here till she is well and strong." She hesitated, swallowed, and after a few moments said, "I will also speak with Jacob. Say nothing of this to anyone, Zilpah. I mean anyone."

Deborah returned to Laban's camp, grabbed essentials, and instructed the servants to move her tent to Jacob's camp. The urgency in her voice had them scurrying from tent to tent. There was no doubt in her mind that Leah needed her. As she packed, she remembered how both she and Rebecca prayed for twenty years before Esau and Jacob were born. She was there when the Canaanite wives of Esau bore *his* children and now, she would be there to deliver Jacob's firstborn. Pain and joy clutched at her heart in equal measure at this bittersweet moment. "Lord God bless her with a son," she prayed. Such prayer leapt from her soul as naturally to her as breathing.

By her return that evening, Jacob and the rest of the household had returned from the fields. Jacob welcomed her in a warm embrace. Ignoring the dirt and sweat that covered him after his day's toil, she wrapped her arms around him and whispered in his ear, "I need to talk to you. Privately." She walked away with Jacob hurrying to catch up.

CHAPTER 39

*L*eah sat quietly in her tent. Barely able to lift her hand, she wiped her face with a cloth. Her hand then collapsed back on the mat as though weightless. She had eaten much earlier while Zilpah explained about Deborah moving in. The thought gave her comfort and somehow stilled the war playing out in her stomach. "Did Deborah mention what ails me?" she asked Zilpah, who was playing gentle harp music to soothe her. Laughter floated into the tent with the cooling evening air. Her ears pricked up as she heard Rachel's laughter, louder than all the others.

She pulled her attention back to Zilpah, who had not responded. "Well, did she say or not?" Zilpah looked at her wishing with every fibre of her being she could be the one to share the good news.

"Deborah will speak with you herself, my lady," she said, turning back to the harp.

Moments later, Deborah entered the tent with a plate of lentil stew in her hand. "Jacob cooked it especially for you," she said as she handed it over to Leah.

Leah grabbed the spoon and ladled the stew in her mouth.

She swallowed but still food dripped down her chin and stained the covers below.

"It's lovely to see you eat again, my child. You will need it to feed your own child which grows within you."

The empty bowl and spoon clattered to the floor.

The hush that fell over the tent was almost palpable. "I'm pregnant?" said Leah, almost to herself. She rubbed her stomach as love washed over her at the thought of this new life. Tears streamed down her cheeks as she prayed to the God who loved her so much that He had blessed her with this miracle. Over the months when her bleeding had been erratic, she assumed it was just like her teenage years. Things had changed when Deborah fed her a mixture of herbs. They seemed to have worked and she did become more regular after swallowing the bitter mixture daily. That was many years ago. She assumed the grief of losing her husband to her younger sister had played a part in her erratic woman's time. But no. There was a child within her; a child to suckle at her breast and continue Jacob's lineage. This child would draw them together. This child would change everything.

For the first time in a very long time, Leah smiled. A smile that arose from the very depths of her soul.

CHAPTER 40

The news of Leah's pregnancy spread like wildfire. Smiles could be seen while laughter rang out at the news that Jacob's firstborn would soon be here. As preparations began for the celebration, the smell of roast lamb filled the camp.

"Jacob, you're a real man at last." His friends slapped him on the back and winked at him.

"A real woman, Leah." Her friends smiled and rubbed her belly.

"Motherhood is the greatest gift. To bear a child is the real mark of womanhood." The speaker shifted the toddler on her hip. He reached out and pulled his mother's hair with a hand sticky with fig juice.

Leah smiled and made faces at him. The toddler giggled and held out his arms to her. She took him and cuddled him close, longing for the day this would be her own child.

The months flew past and and Leah blossomed, ate healthily, took long walks, and even longer naps. She also spent much time chatting with Deborah and the servants. Sometimes Rachel came and sat amongst them. They had learnt to tolerate each other's company.

One evening, she heard a soft knock at her door and opened it to see Jacob. Her face lit up. "Come. Come in, my husband." An uncomfortable silence fell, neither wanting to be the first to speak. Then, Leah felt the baby kick within her. She stroked her stomach and laughed. "I think it's a boy. His kick is strong, feel it."

She pulled Jacob's hand and gently placed it on her protruding stomach. Jacob smiled as he felt the sharp kick and placed his other hand on the other side of the stomach. The baby, seeming to recognise his father's touch, wriggled causing great mirth.

He rubbed her stomach gently and felt the warmth of her body. He looked at his wife and saw the blood rush to her cheeks. They stared at each other in a moment of tenderness before being interrupted by the sound of Rachel's voice as she walked in without invitation.

"Here is the basket with the baby linen you left at my tent. It appears you are more in need of it." She tossed the basket at Leah's feet, cloths tumbling on to the floor, and stalked out. Jacob hurried after her leaving Leah once more abandoned by the man she loved more than life itself.

CHAPTER 41

The sound of the baby's cry rang throughout Jacob's camp. The pain of childbirth could not compare to the joy Leah felt hearing her son scream for the first time. A feeling so deep swept over her that it almost stopped her heart. Love – expected and yet at the same time unexpected. Nothing the others had said prepared her for this level of emotion.

Deborah quickly guided the baby's head to his mother breast, and he latched on and began to suckle. His mouth instinctively pulled at her nipple. Leah looked down at her son, exhausted. Only a few minutes ago she was the one screaming at the agony that nothing could soothe, not even the ointments Deborah used or the potion she gave her to drink. For over ten hours her son had struggled down the birth canal at his own pace.

Deborah looked on; pride and joy shone from her face in equal measure. She thanked God for the safe birth of Leah's son. The birth had been more difficult than any she'd previously witnessed. The labour alone was hard enough, but for Leah it was much harder, knowing her husband had all but abandoned her. Had Jacob lain with Leah more frequently, the birth would have been easier. Deborah busied herself by cleaning the birthing stool and preparing the afterbirth for burial.

Zilpah entered and a smile lit up her face at the sight of the handsome baby boy. "What shall you call him, Leah?" She watched him suckle for a few seconds then reached out and stroked his soft cheek which was warm from the exertion of feeding.

Leah could not tear her gaze away from this miracle that she held in her arms. He looked just like his father; his hair was black like the midnight sky and his eyes a deep dark brown. "Reuben, his name is Reuben." Shifting him in her arms, she whispered a prayer to the Lord. "You saw my misery; you heard my cries and have given me a son. Now my husband will love me."

CHAPTER 42

⚜

*J*acob sat quietly under a fig tree close to the place where he injured himself all those months ago. He had removed himself from the camp and taken the time to meditate and pray. His prayers included a blessing upon his son with whom he grew more and more besotted with each passing day. He saw himself in Reuben. He loved the way he fell asleep in his arms. Since the birth, he had visited Leah's tent most days to see his son, a complete turnaround from his behaviour of the past ten months.

Rachel was not happy with these regular visits and he knew it; however, she did not dare forbid him to stop now that his child was involved. At least not until a few days ago.

That night he had held his son and played with him until he fell asleep in his arms. Jacob tired from a long day's work had also fallen asleep. Leah lifted her son from his arms and placed him on his straw mat to sleep. She had woken Jacob up gently and whispered, "My husband, come and lie here." Jacob had gone with her to her bed mat and she brought him grapes and grains and fed him out of her own hands. He had enjoyed her tenderness and the softness of her breasts, swollen with milk.

He was drawn into her embrace and lay with her, over and over again only disturbed twice by the cry of the baby screaming for milk.

Early in the morning after a restful sleep, he had returned to his tent. Rachel waited for him with anger etched in every line on her face.

"My love," was all she said before she bowed her eyes, turned, and walked away from him. This had been more than three days ago, and she had avoided him since. Jacob began to pray, speaking much more than he listened to God, for each time he stopped to listen, that still small voice always spoke her name.

"Leah."

He didn't want to hear it. Not today.

CHAPTER 43

When Leah discovered she was pregnant for a second time, it brought great comfort. She had hoped Reuben would draw Jacob closer to her and for a short time it had. But after only one night together, Jacob had not been with her intimately since. His visits with his son became less frequent and most times, he chose to only see the boy when he was in Zilpah or Deborah's arms.

Reuben was barely one year old when Leah gave birth to her second son. Beautiful, his hair was much lighter than his older brother's. His eyes were light brown, a feature he got from her. She named him Simeon – God has heard. She thanked the Lord who had blessed her with a second miracle. Gratitude swelled within her heart as her emotion spilled out in words to her Abba.

The months flashed past with the challenges of motherhood being a distraction from her lonely life. Leah was grateful to have Zilpah and Deborah to help her with her sons because some days feeding and caring for them took its toll on her.

Despite it all, she longed for the warmth of her husband. In his arms, she always felt safe, and Jacob had a way of making her world a much brighter place. Desperate for Jacob's attention, Leah languished in obscurity.

Leah took Simeon for a walk around the garden, her favourite thinking place.

"What more can I do to get my husband to notice me," she asked an olive tree. "Even with sons on my hip I am rejected."

She knew Jacob loved children and wanted more. Many more. Her brow creased as her thoughts darkened. She heard faint voices and looked up. Shading her eyes with her hand she made out Mara and Rachel in the distance. This meant Jacob must be alone somewhere.

Leah rushed back to her tent and dumped Simeon into Zilpah's arms. This was her chance to see her husband alone. She noticed Reuben being entertained by Micah; the young servant girl's laughter rang out as he tossed his little ball to her. The camp was quiet with everyone busy, so no one noticed when she slipped away. She had a feeling that her husband would be by the stream where he watered his flocks. Hurrying, she carried with her a jug of wine and a cloth filled with bread and cheese.

As she thought, Jacob was near the well at the mouth of Padan. He was strolling beyond the trees into the fields where the grass was more tender, and the flock grazed peacefully. She loved this man even more knowing how well he cared for and protected his animals. Leah followed him. Her steps were quick, and she soon caught up with him.

Leah took in the surprise on his face before her husband smiled and welcomed her. The smile reached his eyes and he seemed genuinely delighted to see her.

"Peace be unto you, Leah. Are my sons well?" he asked.

Leah nodded her head and lowered herself in greeting. Jacob saw the cloth she carried and raised an eyebrow.

"I brought food for us to share."

A loud rumble from Jacob's stomach broke the silence. In his haste to get on with the day's work he had left home without even a morsel for his midday meal. How did God know the perfect way to provide him with sustenance? Jacob lifted his head towards heaven and smiled. Then he looks at Leah and urged her forward by lightly holding her elbow. They walked towards the shade of the trees, and she laid out the feast before them. Unwrapping her scarf, she placed it on the soft earth as a blanket on which they could sit. Jacob sat down and stuffed the first morsel of food into his mouth. Chewing, he swallowed and coughed, almost choking himself in his haste to satisfy his hunger.

"Will you tell me the story about the angels climbing stairs?" asked Leah. "You started to share this dream with me many months ago. I am eager to hear more." Anxiety slurred her words.

After swallowing once more and then drinking deeply, Jacob cleared his throat. He looked into her eyes to make sure of capturing and holding her attention and began. "When I left Beersheba, I was heading towards Harran and came upon a certain place. It had been a long day of walking and the sun was setting fast." He stopped and stroked her hand.

A tingle ran throughout Leah's body, and she held her breath. She did not speak. She couldn't nor did she want to break the spell.

Jacob continued. "I lay down for the night, using a stone as a pillow, and in mere moments I was asleep." Pausing briefly, he took another sip of the wine from the jug.

Leah, sensing an opportunity, offered him a mouthful of cheese. He ate from her hand and then kissed it.

"I dreamt I saw a long stairway; it rested on the earth and stretched all the way to heaven. Then I saw the angels of God go up and down the staircase and I was filled with awe. Right at the top stood the Lord looking down at me. I asked Him, "Who are you Lord," and He told me He was the God of Abraham and my father Isaac. And then He gave me a promise that the land I lay on, He would give to me and my descendants. When I awoke from the dream, I knew that the Lord was present in that place and I bowed down and worshipped Him."

Jacob paused and drank from his cup. Leah reached over and put some more bread in his mouth, taking time to touch his lips and smile. Her own lips formed a provocative smile and her eyes, filled with passion, sparkled in the afternoon sun. Jacob chewed, as memories flooded unbidden into his mind. He continued the story.

"This place must be the gate of heaven I thought. Taking the stone I had lain on, I built an altar and poured oil over it; I called it Bethel. From that day on, I vowed to make the Lord, my God."

Jacob urged Leah to feed him more cheese. His mouth sucked her fingers tenderly as he took the titbits of food from her. Why was she so interested in everything that concerned him?

He remembered being overjoyed during his second wedding week as he shared stories of his childhood with the woman he loved with all his heart – Rachel. Soft snores indicated her disinterest.

CHAPTER 44

Leah had listened in awe as Jacob told her about his dream, and her faith in the almighty God was strengthened. She loved listening to him talk about God, and she wanted to know more; not just about God but about Jacob too. Everything about Jacob made her heart soar and the more she knew about him, the more she could please him as she longed to do. These moments with him were precious; her conversations with Jacob were often part of her conversations with God.

Leah longed to be holy; she longed to please God, and she knew her husband could teach her how. Her heart's cry was to see peace within her household. She offered up a prayer.

"Give me more moments with Jacob so I may learn more of you, Lord. Let my husband love me, even if only a fraction of the way he loves Rachel."

She hid the tears in her eyes by turning away from Jacob and pretending to choke on the wine.

Jacob smiled as he patted her on the back. He remembered God's promise that his descendants would fill this land. God had promised him that the whole earth would be blessed through him and his offspring. Could it be true? Did the fruits of his loins bear responsibility for the future of a nation? It must be as God had assured him of this.

What a promise.

He praised God for Leah, who had presented him with two sons. He wondered which of his sons would fulfil the promises of God. Would it be from those born already or from those yet to come? A sense of both peace and love swept over him and he was overcome by the fresh realisation of the enormity of God's promise.

He had spent more time with Rachel and yet there was no child to show for their union. It seemed God had closed her womb. Yet with only brief moments with Leah, the Lord had blessed him with sons. Would the remainder of his lineage be through Leah? Looking around he realised there was no one around to disturb them. Jacob drew his wife towards him and lay with her while sending up a silent prayer that this coupling would result in further sons to bear his name.

CHAPTER 45

"The Lord has blessed you with a third son, Leah." Deborah lifted the baby and placed him on his mother's weary chest. The labour pains had started two weeks earlier than counted and the baby had put out his hand first. It had taken Deborah several hours to coax the boy to turn to prevent both himself and his mother dying. Despite strong herbs, Leah screamed both day and night. "Help me, Abba," she begged when she could draw breath. "Please help me."

Laban had come to check in with Jacob earlier in the evening. With Reuben on his lap, he had sat down to enjoy a meal that evening with the rest of the camp. Leah thought the joyous celebration, singing, and dancing may have encouraged the baby to come early and join in.

Laban had lingered for a few hours after the meal, worried about the outcome of this labour which had started early. Drinking wine with Jacob, and occasionally munching on leftover meats, he awaited news.

"They will be all right, Laban?" Jacob's brows drew close together over dulled eyes. "I would never forgive myself should harm befall her." He picked up his goblet and sipped.

"Leah is a strong, woman, just like her mother. My daughter will deliver you a healthy child and she too will come through this."

Eventually, as the darkness deepened, Laban had left.

"Send word when the child is born." Despite his longing for sons, as any man would, Laban loved his daughters who had brought him so much joy.

DEBORAH LOOKED at Leah and smiled. It was apparent she was besotted with her son from his first lusty cry at the moment she had laid eyes on him.

"Your father will be so proud of you, Leah. What shall you call him?" she asked.

Leah closed her eyes partly due to pain and partly to give herself time to think. Tears flowed at Deborah's words. It wasn't her father's *praise* she wanted - it was her husband's *love*. She remembered the time this newest baby had been conceived. That afternoon stood out like a beacon of light in her mind. She had thought they would return to the camp together, but Jacob had asked her to leave much earlier saying he needed to get back to work.

Since then, they had had no time alone together. Rachel had held him close, especially when she discovered Leah was pregnant. Unable to figure out how or when it happened, she had accused Leah of laying with another man. Jacob was quick to defend her honour which resulted in Rachel spending her days in the fields with him and the nights in his tent. Leah shook her head in a bid to shift the memories. She looked down at her son as he suckled on her breast. He had the sweet face of his father which brought her overwhelming joy. Using the back of her hand to swipe away her tears, she looked up at Deborah and sighed. She whispered just loud enough for the older woman to hear, "This is the one that will bond his father to me. My son shall be called Levi." She pulled the baby more tightly to her bosom.

Deborah looked at her, pity shining from her eyes; she wiped the sweat from the new mother's forehead, pulled her long hair away from her face, and prayed to God that Jacob would somehow demonstrate greater love for his first wife. Her heart ached for Leah and the way she was treated.

CHAPTER 46

The months came and went and with the passing of each one Leah came to realise she meant little to Jacob. There were moments in the past where she was convinced he cared a little but those moments grew less and her heart shrank with the enormity of her loss.

He was not openly hostile; in fact, he remained polite and cordial. These were not words she ever thought she would be using to describe her husband. They greeted each other in passing, exchanged pleasantries, and sometimes even sat together during the evening meal. However, few words were actually spoken between them. It was the silence that pained her the most. When she spoke to him, he responded without the pleasure she would expect from a husband.

He was completely different with Rachel. She simply had to look at him and he would laugh. He hung on her every word and never seemed to tire of spending time in her presence. Most evenings they would sit outside together in the shade and talk. Once, she even saw Jacob attempting to braid Rachel's hair. This was unheard of as it was considered a woman's work.

When Jacob travelled to other towns to buy and sell grain

and livestock, he would return with gifts for Rachel - bangles, nose rings, and colourful scarfs. He would also buy gifts for his sons. A couple of times he had brought Leah jewellery but that was rare. As these gifts coincided with the birth of their sons, Leah thought of them more as payment for services rendered than as a gift.

She thought about her three sons, all strong, healthy and blessed by God. They were the cords she had prayed would bind her to him. She had begged God to turn Jacob's heart towards her and for him to treat her well. Was it too much to ask? As the first wife his affection should rightly be hers.

The women's tongues never stopped gossiping about her, or so she thought. She hated her life and many days she wished she could be reunited with her mother, Adinnah. She would have known how to advise her.

Deborah had tried to get Rachel to see reason without success. She had taken time to explain to both women how households were run. It was common practice for a man to have multiple wives and they usually worked out between them how to share both their husband and the household. Animosity often occurred but they still worked everything out. This situation was uncommon.

There should be equality among wives; Deborah had told them both they should each have their set days in the week to visit with their husband. She told them that even when the husband loved one more than the other, he still respected the order that had been set by the first wife. This way peace would reign. With mutual respect and understanding, and everyone playing their part, life would be good.

Deborah had spent hours trying to explain it all to Rachel, using examples from near and far. Rachel had sat quietly listening and appeared to take it all in, then she shook her head causing her long curly hair to bounce around her face.

"It is Jacob's choice to be with me. I cannot refuse my

husband's wishes. I will not now, or ever, resign my fate to my sister and allow her to dictate when I should or should not be with my own husband." With that she had simply walked away.

Lying on her bed mat, Leah stirred uncomfortably. Alone with only her thoughts and a small bird chirping outside her window as company, she allowed her mind to wander. The memories flooded in, from the moment her father commanded the deceit until the time a couple of hours ago when Jacob walked past her tent not even bothering to step inside.

The news of her ill health had reached him already; Deborah had told him herself. The last few days she had been unable to keep food down and now she had a fever. Her husband's lentil stew would ease her stomach and strengthen her, but he had not bothered to send any.

The love of her children soothed her. Reuben now had strong enough legs to go to the fields with his father even if for only a few hours. He loved to pick wildflowers and bring them back to her; she always welcomed them with such joy. It was love like this, even from her little son that sustained her.

Levi had been weaned for months and was beginning to walk. The children often came to her room to play and tell her about their day before Zilpah shooed them off. "Your, Mama, needs rest."

Restless, she cried out to God from the depths of her soul. In anguish, alone and in despair she said, "Lord, I cannot do this anymore. I am tired. I have no more fight left in me. I have no more desire left in me. If he cannot love me, then turn my affection away from him and turn my heart to you, Lord; be the one I hunger and thirst for; be the one my heart cries for. If You will lift this burden of love from within my soul, then I will praise only You for as long as I live. Take away this burden from me, Lord."

She drew her bed covering from her waist to her chest as the fever washed over her and caused her to shiver as she continued to cry out to God. "Heal me Lord and remove this sickness from my bones."

"Forgive."

The voice of the Lord came to her like a gentle whisper. Forgive? She pondered on this. Forgive who? In response, Rachel's and Jacob's images flashed before her eyes followed by the image of her father.

"No, Lord. Don't ask this of me. Leah hung on to the bed cover as though it was the pain in her heart. Bitterness washed over her. If her father's plan had not gone ahead, she would be married to someone else, happy and with no bitterness.

Her father had dealt her a wicked hand for his own profit. Yes, she had cared for Jacob and grown fond of him over the years he had served her father. But never once had she dreamt she would actually be his wife. She could not, and would not, forgive her father.

She thought of Rachel. Leah had loved her and extended the hand of friendship many times. She had encouraged and cajoled her to share their husband equally. In return, she was treated with contempt and Jacob was kept from her even more. She knew Jacob would have been amenable to sharing them. But Rachel refused to allow that. She would never forgive her!

"Forgive. Trust me my beloved."

This time, the words were impressed deep within her heart, stronger and louder than before. Shaking her head in disagreement as her mind turned to Jacob and the tears spilled, she was certain of three things.

Jacob had failed her.

Jacob had abandoned her.

Jacob had used her.

Jacob had allowed himself to be controlled by her sister. He was the man of the camp; he was the head of the household and yet he allowed this injustice to happen. He had allowed her sister to withhold his love from her. They were equally complicit in her misery.

The tears seemed to wash the scales from her eyes. Was this not answered prayers? How had she been such a fool for all those years? This wasn't love. Jacob was the worst of them all. For the first time in all the years she had been married to Jacob, she saw him for what he really was – a man blinded by love to the point of weakness. Could love be used as a reason to be so unkind? Could love be used as a reason to be unfair? Should love be an excuse for a man to lose control of the women in his household?

"Lord, I did nothing to deserve this wickedness and now you ask me to forgive? I cannot." Crying into her hands to stifle any sound, Leah wept while a battle played out in her heart. She did not want to forgive because to forgive them would be to set them free, and she wanted them to suffer just as she had. "Noooooo," she screamed into her wet palms. Then searching her heart, she admitted the simple truth. "I don't know how to forgive them," she whispered.

"Give them to me in prayer."

Leah stood up. She picked up her favourite scarf from the stool beside her, covered herself, and knelt on the floor to pray.

For all these years, Leah had spoken to God faithfully. But none of her previous prayers felt as important as the words she was about to utter. She had a choice to make: choose to obey God and live in favour or choose to do things her own way.

Knowing Jacob wanted sons, her heart had been filled with gratitude to God that she had borne him three. But her heart had also been filled with pride. This had to change if she wanted to live in God's favour.

She hadn't given freely; she had attached conditions to each son by naming them with the expectation of receiving Jacob's love. Yet those expectations had not been met. Shaking from the fever that washed through her body, she fought the urge to empty her stomach. Oblivious to the hardness of the cold ground, she began to pray.

"Dear Lord, here I am kneeling in prayer before you.

My heart is cold and filled with emptiness.

Sorrow has been a constant companion and the bitterness eats my soul.

My bones are weary with anger and I smell of failure.

I am filled with so much pain and regret.

Every day I am unnoticed, I am unwanted, and I am unloved.

If I am to be a slave in my own house, then let me be Your slave.

If You will welcome me into your arms and accept me as I am…

If You will take this shame and turn it around for good…

If You will be my God and fill my heart with Your love…

Then I will serve You.

I will serve them too.

I will forgive them.

I will place my father, my husband, and my sister into Your hands.

Teach me Your ways, oh Lord, and give me Your peace."

After praying, Leah wiped her tears; a wave of heat flashed through her and she started to sweat. Taking the covers off the mat, she lay down and slept peacefully for the first time in many nights.

CHAPTER 47

The next day, Leah was awakened by the sound of Simeon screaming. She rushed outside her tent and across the open field. Simeon, with blood trickling down his knees, had been scooped up in his father's arms. She suspected this had something to do with the rotten old tree stump that she had repeatedly told him to stay away from. "Simeon what happened?" she asked, her voice gentle. He reached for her and she gently lifted him from his father's arms. She cuddled him close murmuring soothing words.

Jacob picked up a soft cloth and soaked it with fresh water from the bucket. He gently dabbed his son's knee. The boy tightened his grip on this mother and screamed more loudly.

"Simeon, don't cry my boy." His words could just about be heard over the sound of the little boy's sobbing. "You cling on to your mother even more than baby Levi." He tickled the young boy's belly hoping it would make him squeal with laughter, but it didn't. Looking at Leah he said, "Perhaps he needs another brother."

Leah smiled at Jacob. "As my husband wishes," she replied,

bowing her head slightly. Calmness filled her in a way she had never previously experienced. With it came the realisation she no longer had the heaviness of heart that had weighed her down for many months. She would be at peace even if her husband chose to dismiss her.

Now she knew that God had both heard and healed her. Her insane desire to be worthy of her husband's love had faded; she no longer felt the desperate desire to be in his presence. All she felt in that moment was hunger.

"You seem to have regained your strength," Jacob said as he moved towards her. "Deborah told me you were sick, but she must have been mistaken."

Leah moved Simeon from one hip to the other; she was disappointed at the anger that stirred within her on hearing his words. It would seem her forgiveness of him needed more work. Still her dark thoughts continued. Would the news of her death have been more pleasant to his ears? The words on the tip of her tongue begged to be let loose; instead she chose to listen to the voice that whispered in her soul.

"Forgive."

"The Lord has healed me of my affliction and filled me once again with strength. Praise be to God who cares for me." She lingered on the last few words, raising her voice slightly when she said *cares*, hoping it would fill her husband with shame. Her husband who had abandoned his responsibility to God and to her. Wanting to scream words of chastisement at him, she merely put the now quiet Simeon down at his father's feet.

At this moment, Rachel had stepped out of her tent and beckoned to Jacob. Simeon ran towards his aunt, who tickled his chin.

Leah looked at Rachel and smiled. "Peace be unto you, my sister," she said as she walked away. She chose to ignore the jealousy that ripped through her as Simeon ran into Rachel's open arms. She had been tempted to snatch her son out of her sister's embrace but shoved the thought deep inside. Rachel was a good aunt. She enjoyed the company of the children and welcomed them. It was *her* she didn't welcome. Looking briefly up to heaven, she whispered, "How many times do I have to forgive?"

CHAPTER 48

Over the next few weeks, Leah had focused on God. She spent much of her time in the garden praying and taught Rueben how to pray as well. Many of the household slaves worshipped idols and she knew that Rachel had also sneaked to the pagan temples with Mara. Those gods didn't speak, not like the God of Jacob did. Those gods taught nothing of forgiveness either. She wanted her son to know the one true God.

Leah smiled, thankful for God's presence and the favour she had found in Him. Since her focus had shifted from herself to her hope in God, the dark cloud she had lived under for so long had lifted. She no longer felt the need to strive. She no longer worried about much and she was once more cheerful, smiling, and at peace.

It hadn't always been easy though; some days the still healing scars in her heart would bleed without warning. Last week, it was the new tunic Jacob had woven for Rachel that had her turning to God with tears in her eyes. Forgiving wasn't easy. She had felt like it was a daily battle; some days she had won and others she had lost. As the weeks came and went, she won much more than she lost.

Leah began to realise that life with God was a journey - a daily walk of trust and faith. She needed to turn to Him every day. One day, Leah had no sooner knelt to pray when she heard a rustle at her outer tent door. She knew her children were outside with Deborah, so who could it be?

Bilhah entered. "My lady," she called out quietly not knowing if Leah was asleep in the inner chamber.

Leah rose to her feet and hastened to greet the maidservant. "Is my sister well" Leah asked.

"Yes, she is well but in her tent with the way of women. But my master lies in pain and I beseech you to come."

Quiet resentment washed over Leah. Jacob needed her now? Because Rachel was unavailable to meet his needs, now he wanted her to rush to his aid. A few months ago, this invitation would have excited her and had her rushing to his side. Instead, she said, "I will be there soon."

She fetched a small pot from the kitchen area of the tent. "Here is some honey with herbs, use it to make tea for Rachel; it will ease her pain and help her blood flow freely."

Bilhah, lost in her own thoughts, took the small pot and stepped out of the tent. She had expected Leah to be more eager to hasten to Jacob's aid. Everyone knew how she craved his attention, but she sensed something different about Leah tonight. The gossip around the camp saying that Leah had changed was obviously true. What had caused this transformation she wondered. Entering Rachel's tent, she heard her mistress groan. She was even more grateful for the honey filled herbs; perhaps this tea would soothe her mistress so she could sleep. For just a moment she wondered if Leah would arrive to care for her master.

Leah knelt down to pray. Before she could utter one word, God's voice came clearly.

"Go and serve."

"But Lord, I want to pray. I am putting you first. I will go to him when I finish praying to you."

"Serving him is your prayer, Leah my beloved, go and serve."

Reluctantly, she rose to her feet and headed in the direction of Jacob's tent.

CHAPTER 49

Some months later it appeared not much had changed. Rachel walked to the fields where the handmaidens had gathered to thresh wheat. Bilhah and Zilpah stood in one corner so deep in conversation they did not hear her approach.

"The baby is only in the fifth month and already giving my mistress sleepless nights. It must be another son." Zilpah's laughter carried on the still air and caused the other servants to look up.

"She is indeed blessed if she bears another son," said Bilhah.

The words pierced Rachel's heart more deeply than any sword. Weeping, she turned and walked back to her tent. How could this be? Leah was pregnant again. She looked at the small statue that Mara had given her; neither it, nor Jacob's God had given her a child. Fear clutched at her heart at the thought of Jacob turning away from her in her barrenness. Then fear turned to anger.

How could Leah have four children with Jacob, and she have none? She had given him her body in abandonment, yet it seemed the fruit of his loins were closed to her. Was he withholding motherhood from her?

Hearing his sandals approach, her heart burned with jealousy. She rushed out to him without giving him time to remove his sandals or take a long draught of cooling water after his journey. She gripped his tunic, pulled him into her tent, and shook him. Bitter tears fell as she screamed, "Jacob, you have to give me my own children or I will die." She released her grip and fell to the ground.

Jacob was furious at his wife's welcome. Pushing her away from his feet, he left the tent and once outside, kicked off his sandals. Rachel, wailing, followed him outside and grabbed his cloak again. "I will kill myself. I deserve my own sons, Jacob. Why have you withheld this joy from me?"

Jacob could not hide his irritation as he was tired, hungry, and thirsty. Not bothering to hide his anger, for the first time, he raised his voice to her. "Am I God, Rachel? Why do you blame me for your barrenness?"

He pried her fingers from his cloak. "Let me be, Rachel," he said. He finished the conversation by walking into his tent and closing the door.

A wave of emotions flooded through Rachel - anger, fear, jealously, and sadness. Jacob had raised his voice to her. Never before had he spoken to her in that manner, not even when she had stolen the jewellery meant for Leah. That day, he had merely smiled, called her greedy, and put the gold rings on her nose himself.

But today was different; he had even shut her out. Was his love for her fading?

Her mind raced. She needed to regain control of this war. Leah had dealt an unexpected hand in this battle, in the shape of a fourth child. She needed to fight back, but how? Scrubbing her eyes, she fought back the tears. It was time to act. She walked into her tent and paced back and forth. Then it came to her, or rather partly came to her in the shape of one of Jacob's stories.

Only she'd fallen asleep before the end. Now she wished she had paid more attention.

Jacob had said something about the promise of God to his grandfather Abraham that he would be the father of many nations even though he didn't yet have a child. And so, his grandmother Sarah had given him her slave to bear her a son.

Rachel's spirits lifted. She immediately ran outside screaming, "Bilhahhhhhhh." When there was no response, she rushed towards the threshing ground. "Bilhaaaahhhhhhhh."

"Yes, Mistress."

They returned to Rachel's tent before she revealed her plan. "I am going to give you to my husband Jacob as a wife, and you shall bear children for me."

Bilhah's face dropped, but as custom demanded, she merely said, "Yes, my mistress."

Rachel took Bilhah's hand and walked her towards Jacob's tent.

JACOB, still furious but understanding his wife's need for a child, looked up and spoke more quietly than he should. "Why do you come into my tent like this," his brows drew together as he took in the presence of Bilhah, "And bring your maidservant?"

Rachel knelt beside him and Bilhah followed suit.

"Here is my servant, Bilhah. I wish to give her to you as a wife. Sleep with her so she can bear children from your loins. Children that will be mine."

Jacob stared at both women not knowing what to say. Eventually he nodded his head, and a deal was struck. Rachel's smile lit up his world and was a balm to his angry soul. Maybe this was God's way of bringing peace. As the women departed, Jacob remembered the story told of his Uncle Ishmael.

God had given his grandfather, Abraham, a promise that he would fill the earth with his descendants. The difficulty with this plan was that he and Sarah were old and well past child-bearing age. Sarah, taking matters into her own hands, gave her servant, Hagar, to Abraham and she bore him a child – Ishmael. Then, God fulfilled his promise and Sarah became pregnant and his father, Isaac, was born. However, chaos had reigned as the brothers were constantly at war.

Jacob missed his father. His wisdom would have served him well. He wondered if history would repeat itself in the form of more chaos. He already had sisters at war; how much greater would this be if their children also followed this path. "Lord God Almighty, look on your servant with mercy. Let this marriage serve only to bring more sons for your glory. Bless the fruit of my loins and the womb of Bilhah to hold and carry for me a son as my gift to Rachel."

CHAPTER 50

The next day the marriage was arranged; a marriage in name only so no feast was needed. The ceremony was short with only a few witnesses gathered in the sight of man and God. The purpose of the union was declared and agreed.

Shortly after, Jacob entered his tent with Bilhah. He lay with her and immediately afterwards she returned to her work. Rachel was, once more, free to take her place in her husband's tent. A few weeks later, Rachel, hearing Bilhah was pregnant, wept tears of both sorrow and joy.

CHAPTER 51

Leah's labour was both sudden and quick. The last few months had flashed past as she focused on praying, raising her sons in the way of the Lord, and the household duties expected of her. When the news of Bilhah's pregnancy reached her ears, she smiled, thankful that at last, her sister would have a child of her own. She had hoped Rachel would mature at the thought of a baby. Instead, she had become even more challenging. She boasted as though she were already suckling a baby with pride, even though suckling this baby would never happen for her.

Holding her new son in her hands, Leah couldn't care less about Rachel. She had four sons born from her own body and suckling on her own breasts. The battle in her mind had calmed. Jacob was free to be with the woman he loved. She would serve God. God had a purpose for her, and God had given her peace. She was not in a battle with her sister, and Bilhah's pregnancy had changed nothing.

The cry of her new-born son drew her attention; this little one was hungry and latched on immediately. The birthing cord was still attached, and he was already suckling with his face not even wiped with the fragrant cloths

Deborah came and sat beside her, massaging her stomach for the afterbirth to come loose. She sang while the servants cleared the birthing area and made Leah fresh mint tea.

Leah, unaware she had drifted off, was startled awake by the sound of Deborah's voice.

"And what shall you call this hungry young man?"

Leah looked at Deborah, then at her son whose tiny fist clutched her finger so tightly. She had been thinking about what to name him, but nothing seemed to suit him. She knew that if she had given birth to a girl, she would call her Dinah after her mother. A boy's name eluded her.

She had named her last three sons at the time of their birth and their names reflected the desires of her heart. Jacob's love. But her focus had now changed.

And then his name came to her, so clear as though God had whispered it in her heart. It came from a place of gratitude, from the place she had learnt to live, from the place she had learnt to forgive, and from the place she had learnt to have faith and trust. "This time, all I want to do is praise the Lord my God so I will call him Judah."

CHAPTER 52

Only a few months later, Bilhah gave birth to a son. Rachel could not contain her joy and rejoiced with much singing and dancing. She was happy that her prayers had not gone unheard. God had answered, although which God she was not sure. The cry of her own baby filled her heart with indescribable love. She placed the infant on her knees with tears pouring down her face. Jacob sat beside her having been brought in after the birth of his son.

Rachel looked at her husband with joy in her heart. "God has vindicated me. Jacob, I cried, and he heard my plea and blessed me with a son." The baby screamed. Rachel soothed him and said, "Dan, your name is Dan." She rocked him gently back to sleep.

A few months later Rachel was playing with Dan outside when Leah passed by with her own sons running at her heels. Jealousy and anger overwhelmed Rachel. How dare she. How dare she parade her four sons before her? Why did she remind her of the way God had abandoned her? That evening Rachel sent Bilhah to lay with Jacob again.

CHAPTER 53

Leah sat in her tent feeding Judah; the long walk in the garden earlier had left her feeling tired, but she needed to clear her head. The birth of Dan had brought a different dynamic to the household. She started to wonder if it was just her own imagination or if, indeed, her sons no longer enjoyed the attention of their father. Only Reuben, old enough to go to the fields and work, spent time with his father.

A few days ago, Simeon had asked for his Papa and she had sent Zilpah to take him over to Jacob. They returned a short time later with tears streaming down Simeon's face.

"I didn't see, Papa."

Rachel had sent them away claiming Jacob was asleep and was not to be disturbed.

Her heart broke for her sons; how was she to explain the reason for their father's absence? Even when they gathered at mealtimes, they were no longer allowed to sit on his lap and cuddle him like they used to. The younger sons used to take turns being bounced on their father's knee and squealing with laughter. But now Rachel always had Dan placed firmly in Jacob's arms.

"Forgive. Trust me. Love. Serve."

These were the words the Lord had spoken to Leah over and over again, and there were times when she was tired of hearing them. Injustice towards her she could bear but not towards her own sons. How quickly Rachel had changed as well, from the loving aunty to the self-absorbed mother. She put all of her time and energy into Dan and ignored her nephews.

Looking at her older sons play out in the field, it seemed like their names mocked Leah. Desperate for her husband's love, she had placed these three boys on the altar of Jacob thinking their presence would turn his affections towards her. It hadn't.

She looked at Judah. Fast asleep, his tiny mouth still gripped tightly to her breast. This son, she had laid at the altar of the Almighty God. Judah's birth had brought peace to her heart and love for him overflowed her heart. But with his birth came another change. It had been more than five months after his birth and still she was not bleeding monthly. She had not lain with Jacob, so she knew she wasn't pregnant. What could this mean?

The last few months had felt like a battle, an unspoken war between herself and Rachel. This time it was over Jacob's love for their children. An unshakable confidence washed over her. Jacob could mistreat her, but she would no longer sit quietly and watch him ignore her sons.

That evening, before the rest of the camp came to sit around the fire, Leah waited. As soon as she saw Jacob approach, with Rachel walking slowly behind him, she hastened over and placed Judah in his arms. She looked directly at Rachel daring her to utter a word. She saw Rachel cower slightly unable to do anything but walk past holding Dan. Leah inhaled deeply and smiled. Today she had realised she was no longer afraid to take her place and stand up for what was rightfully hers

CHAPTER 54

It was a wet morning; the heavens had opened up with rain still falling at dawn. The sound of thunder had drowned out the screams of childbirth. Bilhah's labour was long and painful, but the morning brought another son for Jacob. His cry was loud enough to wake the dead, but Rachel's song of joy was louder still. She held another son in her arms.

Picking up the crying infant, now cleaned, fed, and wrapped up in soft cloth, she held him up to heaven. "Naphtali," she declared. Tears flowed freely and dripped onto her son's face. "What joy you have brought to my heart, baby boy; you've come into this world to bring me victory and wipe away my shame. She bent her head and kissed his soft cheek.

CHAPTER 55

Leah was lost in thought and a quiet anguish filled her soul. Not even the birdsong in her garden could soothe it. It had been several months since her last bleed, and her heart cried out for more children. She had been praying for many months for God to heal her and open her womb.

It took her some months to muster up the courage to share her secret with Deborah. The older woman convinced her not to worry; her body was simply taking a rest. She had told her it was no small thing to have had four strong sons in quick succession. This did not console Leah.

For the last few months, she had been pretending to bleed. Each month, she would hang out her washed fabrics and carry on as though everything was normal. Shame filled her and she prayed earnestly.

"Lord, please open my womb again so I can bear more sons for your glory. Not for Jacob's love but for your glory. Let me be your servant so that your promises will be fulfilled through me." On her knees with hands held high towards heaven, she shivered.

The voice of the Lord came to her and whispered, *"Zilpah."*

Leah opened her eyes and her arms shot down by her sides. "No, Lord, use me. Let me bear the children. How shall I give him my maidservant. Lord, I ask that you bless me instead by opening my womb. Let me serve you myself."

Leah lay on her face before the Lord, pleading her case.

"Give him Zilpah."

God's word remained unwavering. She knew what she had heard and what God was asking her to do but she could not hide her disappointment. "Lord, I thought you would use me instead, why choose my maid?" The familiar feeling of rejection chilled her bones, was God also rejecting her and choosing her servant instead, wasn't she good enough to be used by God?

"My Leah, I love you. Trust me"

The way the Lord spoke her name captivated her heart. *My Leah*. She was precious to God; in her heart she knew it, and she felt it deep within her. God had been faithful to her all these years. Her emotions ran wild within her. Surely, anything of God must be good. Wiping away her tears, she said, "Yes, Lord." She would obey. The promises of God were much bigger than her and besides, Zilpah's children would be hers by right.

A YEAR LATER, Zilpah placed another son on Leah's knees. With a head full of hair and big brown eyes, he was handsome just like his brothers. Rejoicing in the Lord, thanking Him for the blessing of another son, she looked at him with fondness and named him Gad.

She knew that he brought good fortune with him, for it was only a few months after he had been conceived that she started to bleed again. "Praise be to God," she whispered. Leah's heart and home were once again filled with the goodness of God. Rejoicing at the birth of another son in her tent, she danced and sang with abandonment.

How was she to know that when God had told her to give

Zilpah as a wife to Jacob, she would be blessed so quickly with two strong sons? Overwhelmed with joy, she named the newborn boy Asher. "How happy I am! Even the women will call me happy," she said as she wiped away her tears of joy. No more will they call me rejected. No more will they shake their head with pity towards me.

CHAPTER 56

Rachel came and joined the other women in the camp. They were talking and working as babies crawled around them. Zilpah nursed Asher, Leah wove baskets, and Micah and Bilhah saw to the men's clothes and sandals. Leavened bread waited to be baked and a fish roasted on the fire. Taking in the scene of domestic harmony, Rachel waited for Naphtali to wobble towards her; she lifted him and placed him on her lap.

Disappointment washed over her like a river and filled her with unusual sadness. She was thankful for her two sons and for the unshakeable love of her husband, but she wanted more. Sons from her own womb and more sons from Bilhah. Bilhah's pregnancy with Naphtali had been difficult and the birth hard and she had been sick for months afterwards. As soon as she was healed and strong, Rachel had sent her again to lay with Jacob, but no child was conceived. Her prayers to both Jacob's God and her idols were no longer being answered. Asher's birth was a painful reminder to her that she was losing in this war of children. What else could she do?

Reuben running fast towards them signalled the return of

the men, who walked more slowly. It was harvest time. The days were long in the field and the work tedious, sapping the energy from the very marrow of their bones.

Reuben ran to his mother. "Mama, Mama," he yelled as he tugged at the sleeve of her tunic. He was holding a large bunch of mandrake plants in his hands that he had found on the other side of the field. He had picked the freshest leaves, and he handed them to his mother.

"Reuben, these are very fresh and good. Well done, my son," she said as she examined the fresh leaves and thick roots of the plant. He had picked them carefully, not breaking any of the roots and had even dusted the soil away. Her heart was filled with thankfulness at her son's expression of love. "Thank you." She kissed the top of his head and told him to wash his face and feet before the meal.

Rachel was desperate for the mandrakes. The green plants with their fleshly roots were exactly what she needed to help her conceive. She would keep them for herself and not give any to Bilhah. Deborah had told her about the powers of mandrake in helping with conception, but they were hard to find. She wondered where Reuben had found them.

Rachel fought the pride that stirred within her, but her strong desire to give her husband a son overshadowed it. She walked towards Leah and says "Please, can you give me some?" She pointed at the plant.

Silence filled the air as Leah looked straight at her. This was the first time her sister has spoken directly to her in many years. This was Leah's chance for revenge.

"Forgive."

The Lord spoke. Images of all the years of sorrow and heartbreak flashed through Leah's mind.

"Rachel, you took away my husband, was that not enough for you? Now, you want the gift my son has blessed me with as well?" Her voice was loud, and her anger clear. The pain in her heart caused her voice to tremble even over such an inconsequential thing as a plant.

With little remorse, Rachel said, "What if I let you have Jacob tonight in exchange for some mandrakes?"

Just then, Leah saw the men arriving from the field. She tossed the mandrakes at Rachel's feet and rushed to meet Jacob. She stopped to greet her father and brothers who had arrived to share the evening meal with them, then she pulled Jacob aside.

"Tonight, you are mine," and she walked straight to his tent without another word.

Inside the tent, Leah let out a deep sigh. It had been so long since she was in Jacob's arms. Too long. Yet, tonight wasn't about love or romance. For her, it was about duty. Her duty to bear sons. He had shown little love for her and she refused to show him love.

"Soften your heart, Leah, my beloved, and love him."

This wasn't the first time God had spoken to her when she wasn't praying. But it surprised her every time. She shook her head as though to clear it.

"But loving brings pain, Lord." She paused and waited for a response. The room was silent but for the sputtering of the flame in the oil lit lamp. Then she said, "As you wish, Lord. I will love him. Use me, Lord, as you have so many times already." After praying, Leah went to the outhouse, cleansed herself with water, and scented her body with oil. Then she waited for Jacob to join her after the evening meal.

CHAPTER 57

Jacob walked slowly to his tent. He had lingered at the evening meal a lot longer than was necessary. Long after his uncle and the other men had left, Jacob sat playing with his children until they were taken off to bed. His presence a wonderful treat for them; they laughed and ran around their father's feet. Now the night was far gone, and oil lamps were being put out across his camp. Jacob knew Leah was in his tent and was hesitant to go in. The news of his trade shocked him. How could he lose control of his household so badly that his wives were trading him like cattle?

It had been so long since he had been with Leah. He had watched her withdraw into herself and focus more on her sons, as well as finding a new contentment in God. She had also started doing good works. He remembered a few months ago having seen her leave the camp quietly carrying heavy bags and because he was curious, he had followed her. She had entered the house of three widows who had no one to care for them. Leah had become their caregivers.

"Lord, what will I say to her tonight?" he prayed. Realising he hadn't spoken to her alone for many months, he continued praying for wisdom as he entered the tent. What would Leah be like tonight? Earlier in the evening she had spoken to him in a most unusual way. A woman scorned often had many bitter words and he did not have the energy for any such thing tonight.

Leah, sitting down looking out the small window in the inner room, turned to welcome Jacob. She bowed her head, looked at him, and smiled. Jacob smiled back and his heart melted. The presence of God was in this room and upon this woman. He embraced her tenderly before exploring her body and impregnating her once more.

Leah was thankful that God had heard her prayers. Only a few months later she knew she was pregnant again with Jacob's fifth son from her womb. The dynamic in the household hadn't changed, but the way she saw herself had. The fear that had filled her for many years had been replaced by a strong faith in the Almighty God.

When her son was born, she looked at him with a heart overflowing with love. It amazed her how she had the capacity to love each child with all her being. She placed him at her breast to feed, and he latched on quickly. Another hungry son she had thought, so like his brother Judah. She knew that this precious baby was a gift from God, the reward for her obedience when she gave Zilpah to Jacob as a servant wife. She named him Issachar.

She had found it difficult to delegate the responsibility for childbearing. It had given her comfort and joy to be the one who bore Jacob sons and handing it over brought her pain and suffering. Especially since she was the only one of the sisters who could bear his children.

Rachel had her husband's love, but she had his children. It seemed like the right balance of power. Still, she chose to obey, putting her pride and her own desires aside. The reward for her obedience lay in her arms.

CHAPTER 58

Rachel's mood deteriorated greatly at the news of Leah being pregnant yet again. The joy she felt at being the one Jacob loved had started to wane and sorrow had taken its place. Leah's tent was now being extended once again; another curtain of goat hair woven by Jacob himself was being tied to make more room for her already large household. Leah had seven children, and they were becoming a small camp of their own. The boys had grown big and strong. Bilhah would often take Rachel's sons to Leah's tent so they could play with their brothers and many times, Rachel found herself alone when Jacob was in the field.

Her friends all had three, four, or even five children running around their feet. She was thankful for her two sons, but she had craved sons that sprang from her own womb. Every night she had cried out to God in despair. Jacob loved her, but bearing his sons would have made him love her even more.

The heart of the camp was now Leah's tent, and if she wanted to be a part of the household, she would need to accept Leah's position in it. That also pained her. This should have been only her home, yet she knew that if not for Leah, the house of Jacob would have been almost empty. Surely, she thought, two sons would have been enough. She had remembered her promise to give him at least seven sons and had hung her head and wept

Jacob had lifted her off her feet, spinning her around until she was dizzy. He had told her that he wanted a house full of sons, even one hundred if the Lord would bless him with that many. He had wished he had many more brothers and not just his twin, Esau. He told her God had promised him a house full of children. And here she was with not even one son from her own womb. With her head bowed down, she had felt like a failure, ashamed, and annoyed at the laughter coming from Leah's tent.

Rachel remembered crying in Jacob's arms one evening many weeks ago. It had been the same night she had overheard Leah tell Jacob she was pregnant again. She had held Issachar on her hips and rubbed her slightly protruding stomach. Jacob had squealed with joy and rubbed Leah's stomach as well and prayed. Rachel's heart had sunk at the sight of them. She was determined to do more to keep Jacob away from her sister.

When Jacob came to her tent and saw her crying, she couldn't explain the reason for her tears. He had assumed it was the same reason as always, she wanted his children. She had not been able to confess that she was jealous. He had pulled her into his arms, and he had shared the story of his own mother to comfort her.

Jacob had told her that his mother Rebecca had only conceived him and Esau after twenty years of waiting on God. He had encouraged her that she hadn't waited that long yet and that his love for her was not tied to her womb. He was willing to wait with her, and he prayed over her womb on that day and many others. Surely, if God wouldn't answer her, he would answer his son Jacob? So, he had wondered why her womb remained empty and Leah's full?

"God, have mercy on your servant and hear my cry," Rachel prayed earnestly, wiping away her tears.

CHAPTER 59

Leah had given birth to her sixth son in the middle of the night. His loud cries had filled the air waking up most of the camp. Zilpah had lifted the new baby and swaddled him tightly in a cloth before rocking him gently. She turned her back to the oil lamp casting them in shadow and the baby settled. "Shhhh, little one. Don't be afraid," she whispered gently soothing the baby as he drifted off to sleep. She placed him back into Leah's arms as Deborah cleaned the birth tent and the other women began to remove the blood stained straws, cloths, and water.

Leah was tired after a painful birth. The labour wasn't long, but the baby had come out bottom first causing her tremendous pain as Deborah was unable to turn him. She stared at him in awe; his eyes were closed, and he was fast asleep. He hadn't even suckled. Exhausted, Leah closed her eyes. She had a quiet conversation in her heart, and thought, "My God has given me another treasure; he has blessed me with another precious gift. Now my husband will treat me with honour because I have given him six sons." Because of this she called him Zebulun which meant gift.

A few years later, Leah conceived again, this time, God had blessed her with a beautiful daughter, and she named her Dinah after her own mother. Dinah brought so much joy into the camp. As the only girl amongst ten boys, she was a delight to everyone. Dinah had a striking beauty and a smile that held everyone and every heart captive, even Rachel. She adored the girl. As soon as Dinah began to walk, she had followed her older brothers around. Simeon, who delighted in his baby sister was very protective of her. He was quick to pick her up when she fell and was quick to rebuke Issachar when he saw him snatch bread from Dinah's hand causing her to cry.

CHAPTER 60

It was early morning, and Rachel sat outside her tent braiding Dinah's long curly hair. She felt her stomach rumble. This was the second day she had felt uneasy. She called out to Bilhah to come and take Dinah while she went to the back of her tent. She started to feel dizzy and had to grab a tree to stop herself from falling. She emptied her stomach more than once, her head throbbed, and her mouth felt dry. What could this sickness be? She walked back into her tent and gathered some straw; placing her scarf on it, she sat down and clutched her stomach. "Bilhah, please send for Deborah as my body fails me," she called out from behind her tent door.

Bilhah carried Dinah over to her mother's tent and called for Deborah who rushed over to tend to Rachel. She made some tea of mint leaves and honey and gave it to Rachel to drink. When Rachel told Deborah what had happened and the way she had felt for days, Deborah thought and said, "Rachel, could it be the Lord has blessed your womb?"

"Me?" asked Rachel. "Can I really be pregnant?" she asked again as a smile spread across her face. She held Deborah's hands and continued to speak. "The last two months my bleeding has been very light."

Deborah looked at her with tears in her eyes; after all these years, God had heard her. Knowing the women so intimately, she knew that it was only a few days until Rachel was due to have her way of the month, so she said, "Let us wait a few days still and see if there is no bleeding this month, then we will know for certain."

Rachel touched her stomach. The miracle that could be within her womb filled her with joy. "Shall I tell Jacob?" she asked with excitement. "No, wait. Be patient. We cannot announce a pregnancy until it is certain. Keep praying to God, and I too will pray that indeed a child has been placed within you." Deborah rose to prepare a proper meal for her. "You must rest."

The next few days went by very quickly, but for Rachel, it felt like many years. When the time for her bleed came and none appeared, she knew for certain she was pregnant.

When Jacob heard the good news, he fell on his knees and wept, giving praise to God for blessing Rachel with a child in his old age.

Leah stood on the other side of the camp. Jealousy gripped her heart causing her to bend over with grief. Even at the birth of Reuben, Jacob had not shown this much care or emotion for her, and now, Rachel was pregnant, and he sat on the floor crying like one of his babies.

The words that filled her heart were bitter; she would not dare to give voice to them. What a display of affection. Jacob showered Rachel with kisses, and they held on to each other and wept together. She instantly felt like an intruder, even with all their children, she felt like the outsider. When would her sorrow ever end? Looking up to heaven, she said a quick prayer asking God for strength and a forgiving heart.

Choosing to be gracious, she walked over to Rachel and Jacob and joined in the embrace. To her surprise, Rachel turned towards her and pulled her in. She felt the weight of her sister's burden flow through her now soaking scarf; she also broke down and wept.

Rachel spent the rest of her pregnancy resting in her tent and most nights with Jacob. The bond between them grew stronger with each passing day. Jacob was not hiding his extravagant displays of affection. He showered Rachel with gifts, new fabrics, and food.

When Rachel's labour pains started late one afternoon, word was sent to Jacob out in the field, and he immediately rushed back to the camp. Jacob paced and prayed outside Rachel's tent. He heard her cry and scream in pain and worry ripped through his heart. "Father, please save my wife and my child," Jacob prayed as he stood outside for hours.

He refused water, food, or even a chair to sit and wait. He paced up and down outside the tent praying and waiting. Then he heard the baby cry and Bilhah came out. "My Lord, a son," she said before rushing back in.

Jacob had immediately broken into song and dance giving thanks to God for another son. A son from the womb of the woman he loved. Jacob's heart swelled with pride. Finally, after all these years, after all his prayers, after all the waiting, Rachel had a son and the same year he had paid off his debt to Laban.

It had been a long fourteen years of serving him for the hands of his daughters. Now his debt would be paid in a few months, and he could not wait to return home. Were it not for Laban's deception, he would have returned to Canaan seven years earlier. Instead, he had chosen to work for Rachel, and she had now given him a son. Love flowed through him. "My Rachel," he whispered.

He had longed to welcome her and his new son into his

arms. Jacob rushed into the field; he looked among his small flock for a young goat and handed it to one of his servants to prepare it so he could cook a tasty stew for his wife.

Bilhah pulled Rachel's thick curly hair away from her face and weaved it into a tight braid. She wiped the sweat from her forehead and dipped a cloth into cool water to rest it on her head.

Rachel was exhausted after the birth and a small fever brewed. The cool cloth on her head brought welcome relief. Deborah noticed her unease, so she lifted the naked infant and placed him on his mother's chest. She parted the cloth so that their skin touched, and Rachel placed her arms around him. The joy of holding her own son in her arms overshadowed the pain in her body.

She placed her hand on the baby's head, feeling the warmth of his body, and the softness of his black curly hair. He looked a lot like her. "He is beautiful," she said loudly, speaking to no one in particular. The women around her were busy cleaning and clearing the tent.

An hour later, Rachel began to drift into sleep, and then Deborah reached over to pick up the baby and swaddle him. Rachel automatically held him tight.

Deborah laughed. "I will bring him back to feed; I just want to clean and swaddle him in fresh cloth."

Rachel let him go reluctantly; the emptiness she felt surprised her, and she was engulfed by a sudden longing for his return.

Even though she loved her other sons, the love she felt for this one from her own body was different.

Deborah placed him back in her arms, and it brought her instant relief. She held him close, kissing his tiny face. "God has wiped away my tears. He has taken away my shame. No longer will I be humiliated. No longer will I wear disgrace like a cloak on my shoulders." A solitary tear dropped from the corner of her eye, and she allowed it to fall. "Praise be to the God of Jacob who has blessed me with this son. I will call him Joseph." She smiled at her son. She had given him a name that was a prayer to God and a reminder that this child was a gift from God.

CHAPTER 61

Leah took a walk to the other side of the camp where her now untended garden lay overgrown with weeds and shrubs. This used to be her place of solace, a place where she sat and communed with God in prayer. It was also a place where she would come to hide from her misery. The last few years had been better as she had found the courage to speak up to her sister and had drawn close to God so the garden had been neglected.

Everything had been good until Rachel became pregnant. At first, she had been happy for her sister, she truly had. Then jealousy had started to creep in. Jacob was besotted with Rachel all over again, and just like that she faded into the background.

And now, only a few weeks after Joseph's birth, her spirit was breaking under the weight of Jacob's rejection. This time, it wasn't just her; it was her sons as well. Jacob only had eyes for Joseph. The new born infant was doted on. Joseph was bathed in goat's milk, covered in silk linen, and laid on a fine rug with tightly woven tapestry made by Jacob's own hands.

Reuben had already begun to rebel at his father's rejection as he was unable to articulate his pain. He communicated his displeasure with angry words and even once had thrown rocks at the livestock. Reuben was becoming a young man. He was growing every day and desperate for his father's love, attention, and teaching. He wanted things to be the way they were before Joseph was born.

Leah's heart was torn in two as memories both happy and sad flooded within her. "My God, when will this pain end?" The words tumbled out of her mouth as her heart opened before the Lord in prayer. "Help me to live in peace; give me Your peace; I need it so desperately."

"Tell me everything, my Leah."

Leah was confused. What else had God wanted her to say? She had no words left and only wanted peace. She sat quietly, trying to calm her raging emotions. Tell him everything? "Everything Lord?" she asked. An unexpected hint of anger bubbled to the surface.

"Tell me everything, my Leah"

Leah rose to her feet and stamped her foot. "MY LEAH?" She screamed. "Am I really yours? Is this the life you give to those you love? I hate my life; I hate my very existence. My husband detests me, and my children and I have become outcasts in their father's eyes. And my sister…" Leah stopped and fell to her knees. "Oh Rachel," she sobbed. "You didn't have to make my life so miserable; you didn't have to treat me so wickedly. I didn't want to take your place; I didn't choose this life; I didn't steal from you; I, too, was a victim of our father's choice. Why, why, why, did you punish me for this? Why?"

Leah felt the softness of the earth against her face. She thumped the ground willing it to open up and engulf her within it. She recalled a time when she was only seven years old and had a fever that almost killed her. Lifting herself from the ground, she took the corner of her scarf and wiped the mud from her face. "Why didn't you take me then, Lord? Why did you keep me alive to suffer this misery? What good can come out of this pain? What purpose can lie behind this life of emptiness and sorrow? You asked me to forgive; I have forgiven. You asked me to love; I have loved. You even asked me to serve, and I have served with my whole heart. Still, here I am. What use am I to this world, and what use am I to you, God? The void of my husband's love ravages my soul. Just once in my life, I pray to be loved like Rachel is loved."

"*I LOVE YOU with an everlasting love, my beloved. I, the Lord, have chosen you.*"

Leah heard the voice of the Lord in the depths of her soul. A quiet war broke out between her spirit and her soul. Was God's love enough to satisfy? Many years ago, she had prayed for God to take away her longing for Jacob. God had heard and had answered her; so why was she at this place again?

Standing in the garden, her heart and soul exposed before God, she took heed of the invitation to *tell Him everything*. Kneeling down, she poured out her aching heart before Him.

"Dear God, I am sorry. Please, forgive my ungrateful heart that is still wounded within me. You say I should forgive, but each day I feel hurt and betrayal again, so forgiveness becomes difficult. You have asked me to tell you everything, so I will. I am angry, rejected, and ashamed. I feel unwanted, unnoticed, and unloved. I feel used and discarded. Now that Jacob has Joseph, I no longer have any value in his eyes. The love and respect I crave and believe I have earned after the births of my children is all gone at the birth of this child. I feel betrayed by my own sister. Why didn't she just let me share him? She never really loved Jacob herself; she told me so even the night she was betrothed to him. She desired someone younger. So why did she choose to punish me and withhold our husband from me? I lost both my sister and husband in this war brought upon us by our own father."

She stopped and took some deep breaths before continuing.

"And Lord, I detest my father, Laban, too. His wickedness

has caused me to live this life of misery and pain. I would have been better as an unmarried slave. Also, Lord, I am angry with you. Why didn't you make Jacob love me, and why did you take away from me the one thing I had over my sister? Why did you give Rachel a son? My children and I have now been cast aside. Oh, how I wish Joseph had never been born."

As soon as the words came out of Leah's mouth, something that felt like shame punched her in the stomach and she doubled over. She could feel it in her mouth; the bitter taste of the ugly truth that had been hidden within the depths of her heart. She suddenly felt vulnerable before the Lord; it was all out in the open now. She had told Him everything, although she regretted her last words. What kind of a woman was she? Would even God not reject her now?

"My Leah! I love you. Turn your heart towards me and trust me."

A gentle breeze came, and it seemed to bring peace and comfort with it.

She had come face to face with her deepest emotions and discovered they were raw and ugly. Yet, God had not rejected her. His face was still turned towards her. She breathed in deeply and breathed out all the painful emotions she carried. She finally felt freedom. The weight of sorrow had been lifted from her shoulders.

Bowing her head again she whispered, "God, I cannot believe you still love me, even after I have exposed my heart to you and screamed at you. Please forgive me; forgive my careless words and heal my broken heart. Heal my broken expectations, Lord, and help me to let go of the past and truly forgive Jacob and Rachel. Give me love for Joseph; I pray that you bless him and make him more successful."

Peace washed over her as she continued.

"As for my own life, my dreams, and my children, I place all in your hands. Turn my heart towards you my Abba, turn my spirit, my soul, and my body to forever be in service to you.

Please, fill the empty void within me and protect me and my household. I pray for Jacob and for Rachel. Bless them Lord. You have asked me to trust You. I will."

Feeling much better, Leah gathered her things that had been strewn on the grass hours earlier and made her way back to her tent. The sun was drifted into an early slumber. As she walked into the middle of the camp, she saw the other women and the children playing. She carried on praying and asking God to at least show her the purpose for her pain. Just then, Judah ran towards his mother and hugged her.

As she felt her heart beat next to his, she heard God gently whisper, *"Him."*

Leah stopped and looked at Judah. Him? She smiled, of course it would be him. He had been the only son she had given glory to God for, the one whose name meant "Let God be praised."

PART 3

Genesis 30: 25-43
Genesis 31
Genesis 33: 4-5, 18
Genesis 49: 29 - 32

CHAPTER 62

◈

Jacob awoke to the sound of Joseph crying. He heard Rachel trying to settle him and listened to her as she whispered words of comfort. Shortly after, he heard the sound of his son suckling. It was early dawn, and his heart was still unsettled within him. These last few weeks his longing for home had increased. Rising up, with a firm decision in his heart, he prepared himself and made his way to his father-in-law's camp.

He saw Laban sitting outside on a tree stump, talking to his sons. As they heard him approach, their conversations ceased, and Laban rose to welcome him.

"So early in the day, Jacob? Is all well in your household?" Laban asked him with raised brows.

"All is well with my household; my wives and children are resting well."

Laban invited him to sit next to him on the tree stump and waved his sons away. He sensed Jacob's need for privacy.

"Tell me, my son, what brings you to me. I can see your troubled heart within you."

Jacob shifted forward and tapped his feet on the ground

gently. Holding on to his long beard and stroking it for courage and comfort, he struggled for words. They were in his head but somewhat reluctant to come out of his mouth. It wasn't that he was afraid of his uncle, far from it, but he knew him to be a shrewd man. Jacob sent a quick prayer. "Help me, Lord," he whispered under his breath.

This caused Laban to draw closer to him thinking Jacob had spoken to him.

"Send me away in peace, as I long to go back to my own country. I have served you dutifully for many years. Here I sit before you now, asking this one thing of you. Let me go with my wives and my children back to the land of my family."

As soon as Jacob spoke the words, relief flowed within him and a strong sense of longing for home overwhelmed him to the point of tears.

Laban stood up and began to pace back and forth. This news was both unexpected and unwelcomed. Looking ahead of him towards the fields, he saw the abundance of his livestock in the distance. He walked up to his nephew and urged him to rise up to meet his gaze. Holding his attention, he said, "Don't leave me now, Jacob; have I not found favour in your sight? I know that everything I have today is a blessing from God because of you. I know this because even my gods have confirmed it to me, and I have seen it with my own eyes. Tell me, what can I give you as wages? Name it. Anything you say. Just stay with me."

Jacob was surprised at Laban's honesty. There was much truth in everything he said.

He replied, "Yes, you have spoken well. Indeed, your cattle, sheep and goats have fared well under my care. They were only a few when I arrived fourteen years ago, but now, they are abundant. The Lord has favoured you greatly. But what about me? When shall I provide for my own household and have that which is mine?"

"Ok, tell me now, Jacob, what shall I give to you?" Laban asked again.

Jacob paused and thought. Even if his uncle released him now, all he would take with him would be his wives, children, servants, and a few meagre possessions. After all these years, would he now return to become his brother's slave or live off his father's hard work? Sensing an opportunity arising from his uncle's desperation, Jacob looked at Laban and said, "Do not give me anything. But if you will agree to do this one thing that I am going to ask of you, then I will stay and tend the pasture and also keep the flock."

Jacob stopped for a brief moment as an idea formed clearly in his mind. He closed his eyes to hear what the Lord was whispering to him. Hearing Laban pace again, he knew the older man would be willing to listen to him.

"Let me take from your entire flock today all the speckled and spotted sheep, all the dark or black lambs, and the spotted and speckled goats as my wages. These marked ones will be mine and will make for easy reconciliation when it is time to settle my debt completely. If any livestock that are not spotted, speckled, or black are found with me, then it will be clear that they have been stolen. So, in this way, we shall know what belongs to me and what is yours."

Laban looked at his nephew and smiled. "Let it be done as you have said." He extended his right hand towards his nephew. As Jacob grabbed on to it and shook it firmly, Laban grinned. What a foolish man; he only wanted the speckled and spotted ones. He could have asked for so much more.

Jacob was satisfied with this new turn of events. Now that he knew what his wages would be, he could work towards building for himself his own flock and not return home to his father empty handed. Jacob decided to go back to his tent to see his son Joseph instead of heading straight into the pastureland to work.

As soon as Jacob left, Laban put on his work garments and headed into the fields. That very day he secretly removed all the goats that had streaks and spots. He then urged his sons to take all of these and the black ones far away into the land.

CHAPTER 63

A few hours later, when Jacob arrived at the pasture ground, he saw only a few of Laban's flock. He noticed that none of the flock were streaked, spotted, or speckled. The realisation of what his uncle had done dawned on him.

He should have come immediately after the agreement was made to separate what was his from his uncle's. Betrayal and anger rushed through his veins, and he let out a loud piercing scream. The livestock scattered. Falling on his knees, he cried out, "Oh God, do you not see this injustice before your eyes? Will I forever live in the shadow of my past mistakes?" Jacob threw down his walking stick and started to weep; he fought the strong desire within him to curse Laban.

Jacob walked over to the oak tree that provided shelter from the hot noon sun. He sat on a large tree trunk and bowed his head before God. His mind wandered back to his mother. It was his obedience to his mother that had led him here, costing him much more than he bargained for. Running away from the wrath of both his father and brother, he had become a fugitive. Regret washed over him without invitation. He longed for home, to right his wrongs, and to apologise to his brother. He wondered if his father would still be alive.

"Lord, you said that if I serve You, You would make me prosper. Please, do not turn your eyes away from this wickedness that has been done to your servant. Show me the way that I should go so that I will not go back empty to my father's house"

Jacob heard the cattle bleat loudly causing him to look up. "They must be thirsty," he whispered. Standing up, he noticed the branches of the almond tree. He knew just what he must do. He quickly gathered some almond branches. He walked further afield and collected fresh branches from the poplar and plane trees. Setting them in a heap before him he carefully peeled bark away leaving stripes in them which exposed the white underbelly.

He took the striped branches and placed them in the water troughs. Over the next few months, Jacob took time to change the branches each week. The cattle drank, they mated, and conceived, all the while looking at the striped branches in their watering troughs.

When the cattle went into labour, they all gave birth to streaked, speckled. and spotted offspring. Jacob separated the lambs and made them face towards the streaked, dark or black flock when they mated. He also put aside all of his now growing herds, separating them from Laban's flock so that they would not mix with or breed with any of Laban's flock.

He also made sure to only put striped branches in the watering troughs when the stronger animals were breeding and when their offspring came, they were all strong, healthy, streaked, speckled, or spotted. But when the weaker animals were breeding, Jacob removed the striped branches from the watering troughs so when they were born, all the cattle were clear of blemish and weak. These ones became Laban's flock.

CHAPTER 64

The years seemed to fly past with Jacob's prosperity growing. He now had a huge flock of strong cattle, sheep, and goats. His male and female servants had increased. Following the sale of his own livestock, he bought donkeys and camels. God had indeed blessed him abundantly.

Leah leaned over the hot pot of stew that she was cooking outside on the earthen stove. She wiped her sweaty brow and sat down on the raised earth which acted as a stool. Her eyes narrowed against the sun's glare as she watched her oldest sons, Reuben and Simeon deep in conversation with some of the male servants. She called out to Simeon who either didn't hear or was ignoring her. Before she could call out again, Reuben walked towards her and told her that there were rumours being spread about the source his father's wealth.

Leah tasked Zilpah with caring for the food so she could hurry over to Rachel's tent. She let herself in without asking. "I have just heard from Reuben that our brothers are accusing our husband of theft. They claim that Jacob has taken away everything that belongs to our father as his own, acquiring both his wealth and his honour."

Rachel let go of Joseph who immediately disappeared to play outside. "How can they say such a thing? We have seen Jacob work hard all these years. Sometimes I think he cares for the livestock more than us. Would anyone believe these lies?" Rachel asked, a frown spreading across her face.

"How can we know what they will or will not believe? I will leave this news in your ears to share with Jacob upon his return." Leah turned to walk back towards the tent.

Rachel pulled her by the arm. "Why me? Why have you left this heavy news with me? Was it not your son that was told the words; are you not the first wife?"

Leah looked at her stunned and unsure of what to say. Her mind was clouded by both worry for her husband's reputation and anger at her sister's cowardice. Now that there was bad news to impart, her sister was quick to enthrone her as the first wife.

"Fine. I shall be the bearer of bad news then." Leah turned and walked away. "Lord, forgive You say?" Sighing deeply, she resigned herself to her fate to be the one to tell Jacob.

That next evening, she approached him after his meal. He was sitting outside; it looked as though he was praying. She knelt beside him. Unable to form the words she prayed for courage. "Jacob."

Even before she finished calling him, he turned, smiled, and said, "I know, Leah. I heard it with my own ears from the shepherds at the well. Your brothers have called me a thief, and your father's countenance has changed towards me." He rested his head on the wall behind him.

"Rise to your feet, Leah, and sit beside me. You are not to blame for your brothers' words or your father's actions." He opened his hands and stretched them towards Leah, inviting her to take some of the raisins and almonds he was nibbling on. Together, they sat in silence before Jacob began to pray.

CHAPTER 65

The next morning, Leah was hanging out wet clothes to dry when Michael, one of Jacob's shepherds, came to call on her. He left a message that Jacob wanted both she and Rachel to join him in the field. Leah knew it was important as there had been a brooding atmosphere over the camp for some days.

Leah had been praying for days for God to vindicate Jacob from these accusations. Her father's attitude towards Jacob was now hostile, and it had been many weeks since he joined them for a meal. She walked over to Rachel's tent where Dinah entertained Joseph and Dan. Their laughter lightened the mood.

She signalled to Rachel to come outside, not wanting the children to hear what she had to say. She informed Rachel of the summons, and her sister went inside to get dressed. Leah waited for her.

Both women were silent and lost in their own thoughts; Rachel was the first to speak. "Is this how our father is going to destroy our lives again?"

Leah shrugged her shoulders feeling her life had been destroyed the most. What impact would any of this have on

Rachel? Her life had been bliss compared to hers. A vice like fear gripped her heart; this was the first time Jacob had ever summoned them both to the fields together. Whatever he wanted to say would not be good, and she was most likely to feel the full impact of his words. Her hands began to sweat, and her mouth felt dry. She tried to swallow but failed. When she saw Jacob, her heartbeat grew faster and louder. She looked at Rachel to see if she felt the same fear: apparently not, as her sister was rushing towards their husband to kneel at his feet.

Rachel's actions annoyed Leah. Her own fear of what was to come grew more tangible until she noticed Jacob smile at her. Stretching out his hand, he urged her to join them, and together they walked towards the other side of the field. This had been the place where Levi was conceived. She smiled at the private memory and looked at Jacob wondering if he too remembered.

As they approached the overgrown oak tree, Jacob pulled them both close. Keeping his voice low he said, "Will you both bear me witness that your father has changed towards me?"

Leah and Rachel looked at each other and both agreed by nodding their heads, so Jacob continued. "You also know that I have served your father faithfully all these years by working hard for him. He has cheated me many times by making me work longer and harder," he whispered looking at Leah.

Leah felt pain as though a knife had pierced her heart. The pain intensified when her sister also looked at her. She imagined they were thinking that she had been a party to her father's duplicity. Leah turned her head away in shame. Tears filled her eyes, but she held them in. No. She would not cry in front of them. "Help me, Lord."

Jacob must have realised the impact of his words. He gently touched Leah's arm inviting her to turn her attention to him. He pulled her closer to himself, and her heart melted at the unexpected gesture.

Jacob said, "Your father has changed my wages many times,

and it is only by God's mercy that he has not ruined me. If only speckled animals were to be my wages, then only speckled were born. Similarly, with streaked. God stepped in and many in your father's flock now belongs to me."

Jacob paused to catch his breath and give his wives some time to think about what he had just said. He wondered if he should share his dream with them. Making up his mind, he inhaled deeply and continued.

"I had a dream that the angel of the Lord appeared to me and said to me, *'Jacob.'* And I said, *'Here I am.'* And then He said, *'Look up and see, all the rams which are mating are streaked, speckled, and spotted; for I have seen all that Laban has been doing to you. I am the God of Bethel, where you anointed the pillar, and where you made a vow to Me; now stand up, leave this land, and return to the land of your birth.'"*

Jacob waited for his words to sink in. He gave them a few minutes to think about what he had just said before continuing. "Leah. Rachel. God is calling me back to my own country and to my own people. Will you gather your children and your servants and return with me?"

Rachel looked at Leah, and then at Jacob and nodded her head. "I will go."

Leah also nodded her head. Her arms were still held by Jacob, and she revelled in his warmth. She was grateful that the invitation had been extended to her. She shivered at the thought of what she would have done if Jacob had left without her. Deciding to assert her place as the first wife, she looked at Jacob and said, "There is no inheritance for us in our father's house. Now he has sold us for his gain. He has squandered the profit from our sale; we are of no use to him. Whatever God has taken from our father and placed in your hands, it is for us and our children. My children and I will follow you home."

"You have both made my heart full with your words. But will your response change when I tell you this – we will not have your father's blessing. You cannot say goodbye nor can you speak with your brothers about our plans. Will you still go?"

Leah looked at Rachel but did not wait for her response. "We will go." Her tone invited no argument.

Plans were put into place for a swift departure. Leah and Rachel instructed their servants to pack up their possessions and gather their children. The male servants began to dismantle the tents and gather the camels and donkeys. Jacob, still out in the field, pulled together the livestock being careful to only choose the ones that had been agreed upon – streaked, spotted, and speckled.

While the women were busy getting the children ready and packing food, Rachel slipped away unnoticed from the camp. Covering herself with a huge scarf, she carried a small sackcloth and made her way to her father's camp. She entered his tent through the side door, headed straight to the altar, and stole all of his household gods. She placed them in her sack and moved swiftly away. As most of the servants were in the field, there were few people around. She slipped away unnoticed and ran back to her own tent to hide them amongst her clothing.

This would be revenge for everything her father had done to her; he had destroyed her happiness by including her sister in her marriage to Jacob. Hatred burned in her heart as she joined in the preparation to leave. It was as if she had never been gone. Only Leah had seen the look in her sister's eyes, and she knew it did not bode well. She had watched Rachel leave earlier and her heart sank. She knew whatever her sister was up to would lead to heartache.

CHAPTER 66

Jacob had led the way taking with him everything he owned. They had crossed the Euphrates and headed towards the country of Gilead on the east side of the Jordan River. They had been moving for three days now, and he knew that Laban would soon begin to pursue him. It had cost him more than one hundred animals to buy the silence of Laban's servants. They had agreed to give him three days to escape before Laban was told of his departure.

Laban had been perplexed when he came home. His tent did not look like it had been broken into, but all his household gods were missing. He asked all his servants, but none could offer an explanation as to what had happened. Who would dare steal his gods? His sons had not yet returned and so he had to wait a few days in order to speak with them. On the third day, he had been told that Jacob had fled with his whole family and all their livestock.

Laban had been furious; anger coursed through his veins like a poison burning within him. How dare Jacob do this to him. He gathered an army, calling on all his sons, his relatives, and his male servants to join him in the chase. They had moved fast and overtook Jacob on the seventh day in the hill country of Gilead.

They pitched their tents on the hill where Jacob and his family were also camped. The previous night, Laban had dreamt that God told him not to touch a hair on Laban's head. He had instructed his men not to attack Jacob and to leave any talking to him.

Laban, afraid of Jacob's God, approached Jacob calmly. Jacob was waiting outside his tent where he had been waiting for many hours as anxiety held his heart in a tight grip. He expected Laban to be angry, and so not wanting to speak with him in private, he stood outside his tent.

Laban, despite the anger coursing through his veins and thinking he would like to kill his nephew, managed to stay calm. With a neutral tone he asked, "What did I do to deserve such deceit? You left without a word; you carried away my daughters as though they were your slaves."

His voice grew louder.

"Jacob, why the secrecy in regard to your departure? In doing this you denied me the joy of kissing my grandchildren and my daughter's goodbye. What a foolish, foolish thing you have done my boy. I would have sent you away with singing and rejoicing; we could have killed a fattened calf and rejoiced as one. You know that I have every right to harm you, and it is within my power to do so, Jacob. But I will not. I cannot, as your God appeared to me in a dream last night and warned me not to harm you."

He paused and took some deep breaths before swigging water from the wineskin at his side.

"I can understand homesickness and wanting to return to your family. That I can forgive. But why did you insult me further by stealing my household gods?" he asked moving closer to Jacob's ear so that his son-in-law could feel his hot breath on his skin.

They were standing shoulder to shoulder, and Laban could hear Jacob's heart beating. Standing a foot taller than Jacob, he used his height to intimidate. Jacob bowed his head and stepped away from his uncle, aware that his camp was watching from behind tent doors. Jacob knew that God was with him as it was He who had told him to leave. After protecting him all these years, He would not abandon him now.

Anger bubbled up in his chest and gave him confidence. Why was he once again being accused of theft? "Fear that you would send me away without my wives or children meant I fled in secret. But I am not a thief and your accusation burns within my soul. So, I say in the name of the Almighty God, whoever has taken your gods shall not live. Search everywhere and everyone and if you find anything that belongs to you, take it. But I say again, whoever has taken your gods shall not live." Jacob stepped aside and pointed towards his tent door giving his uncle access to search his tent.

Leah's heart skipped a beat as she remembered seeing Rachel leave the camp. Immediately she knew the truth: Rachel was the one who had stolen their father's gods. Before she could even gather her thoughts, her father stepped into her tent rummaged through it, tossed mats aside, and checked every single corner. He hadn't even stopped to speak to her or respond to her own greetings. Finding nothing, he walked through her tent to the maids' room at the back. There the children had gathered. Checking everywhere and still finding nothing, Laban came out through Leah's tent and into Rachel's.

Leah's heart sank, afraid her father was going to find the gods in Rachel's tent. Where could she have hidden them? She imagined the worst – Rachel would be killed and Jacob shamed. She tried to get Jacob's attention, but he was oblivious. Rushing to her own tent, she began to pray.

CHAPTER 67

As soon as Laban had entered Jacob's tent, Rachel had gone quickly to the back of her own tent where the sackcloth with fabric lay tied together. She opened it, grabbed the gods, and threw them into a camel's saddlebag. Then she placed it on the mat in front of her tent and spread her cloak over it. Pouring water on the ground, she used the resultant mud paste on her face to make it look dull. Then she dampened her hair with water and placed mint leaves in an oil lamp.

When her father entered her tent, he stopped and took in her appearance.

"Please, my father, have mercy on me and do not be angry that I do not rise up to greet you. The way of women plagues me, and I am sick with it." She let out a small whimper. Laban walked away from where she sat and searched everywhere else, taking care not to come near her for she looked ill.

Stepping outside Rachel's tent, he was joined by his other sons. They had been searching the servants' tents, the camels' saddlebags, the kitchen tent, and the enclosure which contained the livestock. Nothing had been found that belonged to Jacob, not even an unblemished animal.

Jacob was furious when he heard that the search had found nothing. He walked over to his uncle and said, "What have I done to deserve this treatment? What is my error? What sin did I commit that is so dreadful that you chase me down like a wild dog? If you have found any of your possessions in my camp, place them here before my people and your people, so that they can be the ones to judge between us who has done wrong."

Jacob wiped his mouth; it felt parched. He was shaking with rage as his uncle's injustices danced before his eyes. He had waited years for this moment, and he would no longer cower in fear. The fear of the past few days evaporated, and he was filled with courage – righteous courage.

"THESE PAST TWENTY years I have lived with you and worked hard for you. Nothing you placed in my care was lost. I cared for your ewes and your female goats and none lost offspring - not even one. I did not eat of the rams of your own flock. When your animals were attacked by wild beasts, I never brought you a torn carcass for accounting; instead, I bore the loss myself. You made sure I gave account of every single thing and regardless of when your livestock were stolen, or by whom, you made me pay. I worked day and night in heat and cold and sometimes only had a stone on which to lay my head. This is what I did for you. Is this how you repay me?"

Jacob stopped to catch his breath; he began to pace, searching for cool water to drink and finding none within arm's reach. The whole camp was watching now. Laban's head was bowed, whether in anger or shame, Jacob did not know. Taking a deep breath and letting it out slowly, Jacob continued. "You treated me no better than a slave. You tricked me into working fourteen years for both of your daughters. If God was not with me, this God of my father, the God of Abraham, and the God of Isaac, you would have sent me back to my father empty handed.

He saw my misery; he gave me favour; he protected me today. This is my God's way towards his servant, and you did not conquer."

Laban had raised his head then lowered his gaze to meet Jacob's eyes. For the first time, in front of all those he held dear, Laban felt shame and recognised the injustice in his actions. Laban knew that it was time to let Jacob go and allow him to return home. It was time to make peace.

"Jacob," Laban said his teeth still slightly clenched, "The women you married are my own daughters. These here," he said pointing at the children that had now gathered around their mothers' feet. "These are my grandchildren. Your flock has come from my flock, so that everything you have is mine. But what would I do to harm my daughters or their children? So come, let us today make peace before all, and let us make a covenant between us. Let this covenant serve as a witness between us today."

Laban walked towards Jacob and embraced him warmly. At first, Jacob's hands remained at his sides, unwilling to yield. Slowly, he raised them and returned his uncle's embrace, one which lasted for several minutes. When they finally let go, they walked to the other side of the field. Jacob picked up a stone and set it before them as a pillar. He then invited Laban to do the same before inviting the others to place their stones too.

CHAPTER 68

Leah let out a deep sigh of relief. What a day. All the men were on the outside of the camp working together to gather stones and build a mound. She looked into Rachel's tent and discovered she had not moved. Walking towards the maidservants she sent them to find the children and take them to the stream. Bilhah was also instructed to go. She left with puzzlement clouding eyes. She entered Rachel's tent and closed the door behind her. "Where did you hide the gods, Rachel? I know you took them and lied to Papa." She shoved her sister, who toppled over. Leah whipped the cloth from the mat, saw the saddlebag, and searched inside. There were the stolen gods.

Rachel fell on her knees. "Please, don't tell Papa I took them. Leah, please, don't tell Papa." Tears streamed down her face as she clung to the sleeve of her sister's cloak.

"Rachel, because you sat on the top of these gods, curses may have come upon you." She threw the camel bag on the floor. "Why did you take them? You know the God Jacob worships, so why desecrate Jacob's camp with these worthless idols?"

Shaking her head between deep sobs, Rachel looked at her

sister and continued to weep. "He wronged us Leah, and I wanted revenge, so I took the things I knew he cherished. He was more bothered about the loss of Jacob and these gods than his own daughters." Rachel threw them one by one to the floor. "I hate him, Leah, and I wanted him to suffer." She stomped on one of the statues as though it was her father's head.

Leah looked at her sister and pulled her down beside her. "I have no reason to tell Papa you took his gods. I, too, have suffered from his wickedness. But what's more, I have suffered from the way *you* treated me." Leah paused to see Rachel's reaction before continuing. "Could you not see that I had no choice in the matter; our father would have killed me if I had disobeyed."

At first Rachel had no response. Why had she treated Leah so badly? She wanted Jacob to herself, but could she say this? She took a deep breath and spoke.

"I wanted to be the first and only wife, as I told my friends I would be. You took this from me and relegated me to the place of second wife. I hated you for taking the place that was rightfully mine."

She bowed her head and muttered as though to herself.

"What value did I have if I could not bear him sons? Love was not enough. Many nights I felt no better than a whore, warming his bed and satisfying his lust. Yet you, you had everything I wanted. Everything. Don't you understand? No matter how much Jacob loves me, I am still second to you."

Even as the words came out of her mouth, Rachel knew her burden had been lifted. Why didn't they talk like this many years ago? Jealousy had robbed them of their relationship. And here she sat with Leah with the balance of her future hanging in her sister's hand.

"It is by the grace of God that I hold no grudges towards you. I love you, Rachel, and I forgive you."

They held on to each other weeping tears that were tinged with both sorrow and joy.

Leah gathered all the gods together. "We must dispose of these quickly so no one will see them." She put them back in the saddlebag and handed it to Rachel. "Hide this for now. When it is dark and all the men are sated with food and drunk with wine, we will go and bury them."

Leah was about to leave Rachel's tent when she remembered Jacob's words. She turned and asked her sister, "Did Jacob know that you took Papa's gods?"

"No, he didn't," Rachel whimpered. "Please don't tell him, Leah. Please. Jacob will be so angry and hate me for it. If not for me, then for the sake of Joseph and my unborn child."

"You're pregnant?" Leah was surprised and delighted. Taking her sister's hands in hers, she said, "Rachel, I will not tell Jacob, but you must. Did you not hear him say whoever has taken these gods shall die? Your life is tied to his words, Rachel; he has made an oath under God. Don't you see, whether or not Papa found the gods, the curse will still be upon your head. You have to tell Jacob so he can pray to God to spare you. You have to repent of your sins." Shaking her sister gently, Leah tried to reason with her.

"I cannot tell him, Leah. I will pray to God and ask that you also pray for me, but promise me this one thing, please do not speak of this to anyone." Sobbing, she collapsed at Leah's feet. Leah pulled her sister up and held her as she wept in her arms.

Mixed emotions flowed through Leah and a voice within her screamed for revenge. This was her chance to get her own back, by telling her husband his precious Rachel had soiled his reputation. However, if she did this, everyone would believe every rumour about him. Could she do this to the husband she loved with every fibre of her being? Even if Rachel was stoned to death, the shame and humiliation would not be erased from his household or his heart. Knowing this, revenge held little appeal.

But what about truth? Shouldn't she tell the truth? If she kept quiet, would she not be as guilty as Rachel? But deep down, Leah knew that the urge to break her silence was not because of truth: it was because of bitterness.

"Rachel, something in me wants you to feel the pain I have felt these past twenty years." Leah's tears flowed freely mingling with her sister's and she could not still the war within her heart. "Oh God, please help me."

The noise of singing and dancing could be heard from outside, and the smell of roasted goat filled the air. Leah and Rachel continued to sit in tearful silence. Leah finally spoke. "I won't tell Jacob; I promise you this. But Rachel, you must tell him, or you may die. You know the power in Jacob's words comes from God himself. Please Rachel, tell him even if only for the child you carry. If you must, wait until our father has gone, but do it."

Rachel shook her head. "I cannot do this thing you are asking, Leah; if I do die, let me die with honour, holding close to my heart my husband's love and respect."

CHAPTER 69

Laban placed the last stone on the mound. He called it Jegar-Sahadutha, which meant a monument of testimony. Jacob smiled and also called it Galeed which meant witness. "May this monument be a witness, a reminder of the oath taken between us today. May it also be a Mizpah, a watchtower, so that your God will watch over us while we are far apart."

Laban drew closer to Jacob, his smile absent. Looking his nephew straight in the eye, he said, "Jacob, if you should bring any harm to my daughters, remember this mound and remember that the God of your father is a witness between us." Laban pointed at the stones in front of them. "Let us not pass this mound in either direction to bring harm on each other. Swear this on your God and my gods."

Jacob nodded his head. "I swear by the God of my father Isaac." Jacob whispered rejecting Laban's false God's in the process.

Jacob called for a large male ram and offered it as a sacrifice to the Lord. He slit the animal's throat, spilled the blood on the ground, and bowed in prayer to his God. Peace at last, freedom at last, and joy at last. The feasting lasted throughout the night.

The next morning, Laban and his relatives arose early. He called his daughters and his grandchildren, embraced them, and kissed them all. He shook Jacob's hand one last time and then drew his nephew into a warm embrace. "Look after my daughters, Jacob," he whispered. Then he left.

CHAPTER 70

Jacob sat amongst his sons as they shared a meal together. Joseph sat next to his father. Jacob watched as Rachel and Leah talked and laughed together. The last time he had seen them like this was the evening of his arrival in his father's camp, probably gossiping about the handsome relative who had arrived so unexpectedly.

There was something beautiful about seeing his wives like this. He was suddenly filled with remorse and regret. He played no part in bringing these women together, yet as the head of the home, he knew it should have been his responsibility. Love could not be an excuse for neglect; it was difficult for him to admit it, but he had neglected Leah.

Each time he prayed for his family, God had reminded him about Leah, but he had never listened. He allowed Rachel to dictate what he did. Unable to breath as strong emotions swept through him, Jacob coughed and tried to clear the lump that was forming in his throat. Was this the taste of guilt that gnawed at him? "Lord forgive me; I have been a fool both as a man and a husband. Thank you for bringing peace to my home."

The younger boys started to run around, and he looked

across at his four older sons now men in their own right. Soon marriage would come, and his family would grow. He looked over again at Rachel; her stomach swelled with another child. God had been faithful to him, more faithful than he deserved. Jacob closed his eyes, drowned out the noise, and prayed quietly to God.

There was much on his heart, so much more than his wives. Soon he would come face to face with his past. He would see Esau.

CHAPTER 71

*J*acob sent messengers with gifts to the land of Seir in Edom, his brother's land. These were to appease him. The angel of God had met with him a few days earlier, a sign of reassurance and protection from God. Now he needed protection from his brother and his heart was filled with fear. The messengers he sent to his brother returned the night before, telling him that Esau was coming to meet him with four hundred men.

Jacob, who was distressed and afraid, split his camp in two. If Jacob attacked them, half the camp would have been able to escape. He prayed.

"O God of my father Abraham, God of my father Isaac, Lord, it is You who said to me, 'Go back to your country and your relatives, and I will make you prosper. I am unworthy of all the kindness and faithfulness you have shown your servant. I had only my staff when I crossed the Jordan River, but now I have become two camps. Save me, I pray, from the hand of my brother Esau. But you have said, *'I will surely make you prosper and will make your descendants like the sand of the sea which cannot be counted.'*"

Jacob prayed into the night.

CHAPTER 72

Leah placed a cool cloth on Rachel's head. Her body burned with fever, and the herbs they had given her didn't seem to help. They had arrived safely and were now settled in the land of Shechem.

The reunion between Jacob and Esau was one of joy. Despite Jacob's fear, when they finally met Esau, he showed only elation. He kissed and hugged his brother and welcomed them all. Leah had stared at Esau finding it difficult to imagine they were twins. They looked so different.

Rachel's pregnancy had grown, but Rachel had fallen sick and wasn't getting better. Leah looked around her. This city looked and felt foreign and she didn't like it much. Jacob had bought a piece of land from Hamor, the chief of the land, and all their tents were now pitched securely.

Her tent was placed right next to Rachel's, and Jacob's tent was in front of both their tents, forming a simple triangle. The remainder of the tents formed a circle allowing for a social area in the middle. Many nights there was feasting, drinking, dancing, and singing.

Jacob's attitude had changed towards her. It felt like

answered prayer as she now had his respect as well as his attention, even if Rachel still held his love. She was content. God had been so gracious towards her, restoring her sister to her as well as her husband. Their children lived in peace; there was no longer strife in the camp.

"Can I have some water please," Rachel's voice was hoarse. Leah fetched the water for her and then went to find Deborah.

Although old in body, Deborah was still young in spirit. She had insisted on coming with them instead of staying in Paddan Arram. The journey had been hard on her, but she had recovered quickly and was now at the back of her tent hanging out clothes.

"I am worried about Rachel; her pain is severe and her fever ravages her. What else can we do to ease her pain?" asked Leah.

Deborah put the clothes aside and stretched to ease the ache in her back. "I know that God has restored your sister to you. God will heal her. Fear not. Come now, let us go and make some more herbs. I will also find for her some lavender plants which she loves, to lift her countenance."

CHAPTER 73

As soon as Dinah saw her mother and Deborah walk towards the other side of the camp, she picked up her outside cloak and scarf and headed into the city unescorted. Knowing this was forbidden, she still seized the opportunity to go and visit with the girls of the land.

It was so boring being the only girl in a household of all those men. There was no one of her age to talk with and she was tired of running after ten older brothers. Joseph, the youngest was now old enough to go to the fields with his brothers. This left her alone in the camp with no one but the older servants to talk to.

She walked quickly. Having seen the girls many weeks ago, she knew exactly where she could find them.

Shechem, son of Hamor, the sheik of the land, was also walking towards the city. Hearing joyful singing, he turned his head. He saw her long before she saw him. He could see that she was young but also beautiful and shapely; he felt an immediate longing for her.

He stepped behind a tree and hid as she approached. As soon as she had passed in front of him, he grabbed her from behind and placed his hand over her mouth. He removed his turban and tied it around her face. Holding her arms tightly, he tossed her small frame over his shoulder and ran the short distance to his house. He took her straight to his room and defiled her, paying no heed to her tear-stained screams.

Once Shechem had satisfied his lust, he removed the turban from her face and immediately fell in love. "Please don't cry. I am sorry for what I have done to you. I love you." He continued to whisper endearments and stroked her hair in an attempt to soothe her. The minute he let go, she ran from his room and straight back to her father's camp.

Shechem confessed his sin to his father, who lashed out at him in his anger. He begged him to get the young girl for him as his wife.

CHAPTER 74

*L*eah knelt down to pray when Dinah walked in with tears in her eyes. When she had told Leah what happened, she started to scream loudly until a small crowd gathered just outside her tent. Leah, despair clutching at her stomach, held her daughter and sobbed out a prayer. "Oh my God, where were you when this evil happened? Where was your hand to protect her?" Leah screamed, threw herself on the floor, and wept bitter tears.

Dinah sat at the far end of the tent and covered her face with her scarf. Shameful tears poured from her eyes and pain filled both her heart and her soul. Taking her cloak, she covered the dried blood that had trickled down her legs, then she bent her head and sobbed harder.

Jacob was sitting with Rachel in her tent when Bilhah told him the news. He rushed to his daughter and held her in his arms. When she recounted the story to him, anger threatened to explode from every pore in his body. It was still daylight; his sons would not be back from the field for a few hours. How would he tell them? Jacob decided to wait until they returned. Recounting this tale would be more than he could bear.

Just then, Michael, Jacob's servant, came to inform him that Hamor was waiting outside his tent to see him. Jacob went to meet Hamor barely able to contain his rage. However, custom dictated he must welcome this visitor to his household. Before they were able to speak, he heard an almighty rumpus. Looking out of the tent, he soon realised that his sons already knew.

Simeon was furious; he was leading the men as they ran from the fields like a pack of lions.

Hamor immediately cowered behind Jacob, using him as a shield. Jacob held his right hand out to signal his sons to stop. Out of breath and filled with anger, Simeon dropped to the ground and began to weep. Their raised voices - cursing, swearing, and talking at once - could be heard throughout the land. Hamor tried to speak but was drowned out by the sound of noise and silenced by the sheer level of rage.

Finally, Jacob was able to bring his sons under control and allowed Hamor to speak. "The soul of my son is troubled within him as the love he holds for your daughter plagues him. Please, give her to him as a wife." He turned to the sons of Jacob and continued, "Also, take our daughters as your wives and give us yours; in this way, you can live in peace with us. We will open our country to you, and you will live alongside us. There would be opportunities to do business here, and you could acquire property." Hamor hoped that this invitation would be welcomed and would make up, in some small way, for the wrong his son had done to this family.

Shechem was heard from behind them. They all turned at the sound of his voice and he knelt before Jacob.

Simeon launched himself at Shechem; his axe in his hand. Reuben grabbed him before the axe made contact with the young man's head. "Should we lose you to execution?"

Shechem pleaded with Jacob and his sons.

"Please, let me find favour before you. Anything you ask of me I will give to you. Demand from me a very large bridal payment, and I will pay it. Only please, give me your daughter and your sister to be my wife."

Reuben gathered his brothers and they spoke amongst themselves in quiet voices. Then he walked towards Shechem and stood before him and his father.

"We have heard your request, but we cannot do what you are asking. We cannot give our sister to an uncircumcised man. Doing so would bring disgrace to my father and this household. However, if you agree to this one condition, if you and every male in this city will be circumcised, then we will give you our sister to marry. We will also take for ourselves the daughters of this land and give you our daughters as well. We will live with you and we will become one people. But if you decide not to be circumcised, then we will take our sister and leave."

Hamor listened to their words and pulled his son aside so they could talk in private. Could they agree to these conditions? The fire burning in his loins urged Shechem to do so. His father, angry and ashamed of the dishonour his son had brought on him said, "If you love this woman, as you say you do, I will allow this to happen in my land."

Shechem nodded and grabbed his father's tunic. "Yes, this is my desire."

Hamor pried his son's hands from his clothing, turned to Jacob and said, "We will do this. Arrange for the marriage and we will start the circumcision." He pointed at his son. "He will be first."

CHAPTER 75

That night, Leah sat with her daughter as she attempted to soothe her to sleep with songs. Earlier in the evening, she had tenderly bathed her daughter with a wet cloth and a bowl of fragrant water. Her eyes were heavy with tears as she wiped away the blood from her precious daughter's legs. Dinah's cloak was muddy and torn, and she had bruises all over her neck and back. What kind of monster would do this to a young girl?

Dinah placed her head on her mother's lap and closed her eyes tightly; she tried to shut out the memories that were sure to haunt her for life. "What will become of me now, mother?" she asked, her voice barely above a whisper.

"Your father and brothers have agreed for you to marry him. They will give you to Shechem as a wife."

Dinah gripped her mother's scarf tightly around her and started to weep. "No, mother, let me die instead. I cannot marry that man; please, don't let them give me to that man." Wide awake once more, tears fell down her face, and she clutched at her mother.

"Hush now my child. My heart bleeds as red as yours. I wish

there was another way, but this is the only way to secure your future so that you do not remain like an outcast in your father's house. No other man would marry a woman who has been defiled, a woman without honour." The words tumbled from her mouth as if haste would blunt their truth. Leah's heart had broken along with the life she had dreamt of for this daughter that she loved with all her heart.

This was not what she had planned for Dinah; this was not the life she wanted for her daughter. She didn't want her daughter forced into a marriage with the man who raped her and treated her like a common prostitute. When Dinah was born, Leah had prayed for God to bless her with a man who loved her like Jacob loved Rachel: a man who would honour her, cherish her, and fetch a huge reward for her father.

She had prayed to God to give Dinah the life that she didn't have, and she believed in her heart that God had heard her. "Oh God, where were you when this happened? Where were you? God, won't you speak now? I have served you; I have obeyed you; I have loved you. What is my prize? Why did you leave my daughter, Lord? Why did you leave her?"

"I was with her Leah. I never left her."

Leah looked up as though she could see God. His words cut through her soul. "If You were there, Lord, why didn't you strike him dead before he touched her? Oh my God. Who can ever understand your ways?"

Dinah sat up; she placed her hand on her mother's lap. "Mother let me be a servant in my father's house. Please, don't let me marry that man. I know that the decision does not lie in your hands but I would die first before I marry him."

Leah looked at Dinah and was unable to speak. She saw the fear in her eyes and knew that Dinah spoke words that came from deep within her heart. Leah understood her daughter's pain; it was the type that made death look more appealing. She had been there. She remembered the morning after her wedding to Jacob when she too wanted to take her own life. Praying quietly again, she turned her heart towards God. "I don't know if I can ever forgive you or even continue to worship you as my God if my daughter chooses death. Please, don't make her choose; please, don't make her choose."

Leah closed her eyes and decided to do anything she must to protect her daughter from marrying Shechem. If that was the young girl's wish, she would make sure of it. Her own mother was dead when she married, so was unable to help prevent her father's plans. She was very much alive and would protect her daughter with her heart and soul.

So many times she had wished she was a slave in her father's house, so she knew exactly how Dinah felt. This would be a kinder fate than to be the wife of that monster. A man who would treat a woman so badly, and had no control over his urges, would make a wicked husband.

CHAPTER 76

Three days later, Jacob was in the field when two of his servants came to tell him what his sons had done. Simeon and Levi had killed Hamor, Shechem, and massacred every other man in the city of Shechem. His other sons then joined in and stole everything it was possible to steal - their wealth, their wives, and their children. They had left nothing behind in the walled city.

Jacob fell on his knees and put his hands on his head. Only then did he understand why his sons had insisted that all the men of the town be circumcised. This had been their plan all along; they had no intention of giving Dinah to Shechem. Although Jacob had been devastated about Dinah being defiled, he had been willing to give her to Shechem as a wife. Making her Shechem's wife would protect her honour and ensure she did not end up without a husband. Although painful, it had seemed like the only way out.

Most women who were defiled were then rejected by their fathers and many ended up as temple or street prostitutes. He had taken solace that this would not be Dinah's fate because the man responsible for her misfortune was willing to marry her.

Now, his sons had killed him. What would the other men in the land do to them in return?

Fear rushed through him and chilled his bones. "What have these boys done?" he asked. Then he put his head in his hands and prayed.

CHAPTER 77

*L*eah was sitting with Rachel; she was weaving reeds, while Leah was weaving fabric. They were talking about everything that had happened over the last few days. Rachel had recovered fully from her sickness, much to Leah's delight. They talked as they worked. Leah was making a blanket for the new baby her sister carried. Dinah had refused to join the women of the house for the last three days. Her sorrow and affliction grew greater with every passing day. Leah told Rachel how the fear of marrying Shechem had kept Dinah awake most nights.

"I would marry him and then kill him with poison," Rachel said, spitting on the floor to show her displeasure.

Leah laughed for the first time in days at her sister's harsh words. "Would you have the heart to do such evil?" she asked.

"Yes."

Before Leah could respond, Micah, one of the servant girls rushed up. "They are dead. They are all dead. Simeon and Levi killed them all." Panting heavily, the young woman tried to draw in air and recover her lungs after running a long distance. She stuttered as she tried to continue. "I was in the city buying flour when I saw them; they carried knives and walked quietly towards the walls and entered into the city. Then I heard the screams and rushed to see what was happening. They killed Shechem, chopping off his manhood and his head. And then, they ki... ki... killed..." She struggled to continue as tears filled her eyes.

Loud cheering and shouting echoed through the camp and everyone ran from their tents. Leah looked up to see their sons with their arms full of possessions and a long line of women and children trailing behind them. She could not speak.

"Our sons have avenged their sister's honour; blessed be the name of the Lord." Said Rachel as she broke out into song and dance.

Leah pitied the women and children she saw walking towards the camp. Yet, a smile spread across her face. Dinah would be happy again.

CHAPTER 78

Jacob walked back to his camp and met his sons talking amongst themselves. The eyes of the women haunted him as he walked through the midst of them.

Jacob turned his attention to Simeon and Levi. "What is this you have done? You have ruined me and made me an enemy to the people in this land. Don't you know that they are more than us? I only have a few men, but they are many. The Canaanites and the Perrizzites will come together as one and attack me, then I will be destroyed, as will my household including you and your mothers."

Levi looked at his brothers and then he came forward to speak on their behalf. "Father, we cannot allow them to treat our sister like a prostitute." He hissed his words through tightly clenched teeth. Simeon stared at his father, tears running down his cheeks; he moved his blood-soaked sword from one hand to the next without saying a word. His eyes seemed to be daring his father to speak more.

Dinah heard what had happened and ran outside the tent falling at Simeon's feet. He dropped his sword and then picked her up in his arms and took her back to his mother's tent. The other sons from Leah's womb followed behind.

That same night, as Jacob laid his head to sleep, God said to him, *"Go up to Bethel and live there, and make an altar there to God, who appeared to you when you fled from Esau."*

The next morning, Jacob woke the camp, which now included the wives and children of the men his sons had killed. He instructed them to hand over all their gods as well as their charms. They went to their tent and soon returned with their arms full of the objects he requested.

Jacob prepared his camp to move on. He felt this was the only way to ensure the safety of his household. Much of the plunder which came from Shechem had to be left behind. On their way Jacob buried the objects under the oak tree near the city of Shechem. They then journeyed on towards Bethel.

Leah prayed to her God. "Protect us Almighty God, from the evil that surely awaits us on the journey ahead."

In answer to her prayer, the Lord God send a great terror to the cities around Shechem, meaning Jacob and his family were not pursued.

CHAPTER 79

They arrived safely at Luz and took time to rest there. Jacob built an altar for the Lord and called it El-Bethel. Leah sent word to Jacob who was still worshipping God at the altar to come quickly.

"Deborah has died," she told him on his return. She had been sick for many days as old age had come upon her, but it was still a shock. Leah held her in her arms and wept for this woman who had been a rock for her; every time she cried, this woman had cried along with her. She had been there when all of her children had been born.

Rachel held her growing stomach and wept loudly. "What about this child? Deborah, you didn't wait to see this one."

The news of Deborah's death spread around the camp, and there was great mourning as she was loved by many.

Jacob came to see Deborah's body, and he wept. He had known this woman his entire life. She had been there when his mother was born and when she died. She was there when he was born. She had travelled to Laban's camp to inform him of his own mother's death and remained to care for him. Grief choked him, and he couldn't speak.

After the burial rites were performed, he and his sons buried Deborah's body underneath the huge oak tree just below Bethel. Everyone gathered around the tree to weep for this woman, known as the mother of the camp. Jacob named the place where she was buried *Allon – bacuth* which means Oak of weeping.

CHAPTER 80

During the journey Jacob had a powerful encounter with God where he was given a new name, *Israel,* and a promise of greatness. Jacob held God's words and promises close to his heart. He shared some of the vision with his wives that included the promises of God that there would be great nations and Kings from his household. He also informed them of his new name.

They journeyed towards Ephrath, pitching their tents and forming a camp when they needed to rest. Rachel lay beside Jacob in his tent. They had spent the last few nights together with Rachel clinging tightly to him and weeping each night. Guilt of her own deceit plagued her.

"What is wrong, my Rachel? What has you so sad?"

She refused to speak and would only pray to God. Her body was weak and tired. The time for her birth was drawing close and yet again a fever had come upon her. Jacob laid his hands over her and began to pray to the Lord. "Heal her, oh God. Restore her strength so she may not only bear the child within her but also live to nurse it." She shivered, and then cried out in pain.

"Call on the nurse and my sister. Let me go to the birthing tent because the child within me begs to come loose." She cried as she spoke. She had no strength and was unable to lift herself to her feet.

Jacob called out to Leah who rushed over at the sound of his voice. Together, they lifted Rachel and helped her towards the birthing tent. By this time, the midwife, Bilhah, and Zilpah had already gathered. They took Rachel from Jacob's arms and led her into the tent, placing her gently on the birthing stool.

The pain of childbirth ravaged her already weak body causing her to suffer greatly with so much agony. She began to breathe deeply and slowly. Leah rushed out of the tent weeping. She could see the life flowing out of her sister and could not bear to watch. She looked up to the star filled sky and said, "Spare her, Lord. Please, spare her life beyond the birth of this child. Have mercy on her and forgive her, Lord; please spare her." Leah fell on her knees, rocking from side to side as though in a trance while continuing to plead for her sister's life.

The memories of the stolen idols rushed in and she wondered if this was her sister's punishment. "No, she can't die Lord. We prayed; we buried the idols; we fasted; we did everything we could." Leah screamed her pain into the empty night as the sound of her sister's cries brought sadness to her soul. She fell flat on her face before the Lord and continued to pray.

Rachel could feel her son coming and held her breath. She closed her eyes and fought through the pain. She saw death, immediately recognised him, and stared him in the face. She had seen him in her dreams a few nights before and had prayed to God to spare her and allow her to see her son. She shivered again as pain ripped through her, and she let out a loud scream with all the breath she had left. This encouraged the child to arrive. The midwife caught the boy in her arms as he shot out, "Don't be afraid, Rachel. All is well. You have another son." She quickly placed the boy on his mother's chest.

Rachel breathed deep and fast and it was obvious her life was fading. "His name….his na… Ben-oni …." And then she closed her eyes.

The midwife screamed and Leah picked herself off the ground and ran into the tent.

Rachel was dead.

CHAPTER 81

For many days after Rachel's death, Leah was unable to speak. She wore her grief like a heavy cloak around her neck as they journeyed towards Jacob's home. Jacob's grief was tangible. He wept without shame and refused to eat for days. Leah had tried her best to comfort him, but neither her food nor her body was able to satisfy the void Rachel had left in his heart.

Rachel was buried along the way. Jacob set a pillar on her grave. Day and night, he carried his son who he renamed Benjamin which meant son of my right hand, rather than Benoni which meant son of my sorrow.

When they arrived at Eder, they pitched their tent and rested for many weeks. In all that time, Jacob had spent every single night in Leah's tent. They had also spent many hours talking. One night, she asked Jacob to talk to her about Rachel, giving him permission to grieve with her. Jacob broke down and he cried, sharing all the feelings he had held within him, unable to do anything with them but pray them out to God. Leah listened patiently, without jealousy or envy; she let him pour his heart out to her.

Then she spoke; she told him how much she grieved her sister, too. The last year had been special between them, but she grieved for all the years they wasted waging war. She grieved for all the years they would no longer have together. They held each other and cried.

Then she summoned the courage she had lacked for months and asked him, "Jacob, what would have happened to me if I had stolen my father's gods? Were the words you spoke that the thief would die a curse from heaven?" She waited with bated breath for Jacob's response.

"Why do you ask this, Leah? Did you take the gods?"

"No. No, I didn't. I just wondered at the power of your words," she reassured him quickly.

Relieved, Jacob lay back on the mat and chuckled. "What power do I have, Leah, to bring life or death? Only God has this power. No, my words were not meant as a curse. I know how much your father cherished those idols; they had been given to him by his own father and his father before him. Above all Laban's possessions, those gods were the things he cherished the most. I was just giving him permission to mete out justice at his own hands."

Leah shuffled in the bed and he moved closer to her. She encouraged him to continue.

"Death would have come from your father's sword not my words, Leah. Besides, I knew that no one in my household would do something so wicked and evil because it would have caused me great shame. I praise God that I was vindicated."

Relief washed through Leah's body like cool water on a hot night. Leah was glad that Rachel did not die as a result of Jacob's curse. Hearing Jacob's words, she now understood why Rachel did not want Jacob to know of her sin; she vowed to take her sister's shame to the grave.

Jacob turned his face toward Leah. "I am so sorry, Leah. All these years you have loved me, you have cared for me, you have never turned your heart away from me, and I failed you. I cast you aside and discounted your needs and ignored your tears. Please, forgive me."

Leah let the tears flow freely as her heart was overwhelmed with many emotions. He wanted her forgiveness. "Jacob, why do you ask for something you already have? I forgave you many years ago. The grace of God sustained me and continues to sustain. I have loved you from the very beginning, and I will continue to love you all the days of my life. I may never have your love as I am not your *Rachel*, but I am grateful for your acceptance and for your respect."

Jacob drew her into an embrace, and they shared their first night of deep intimacy; it was a night like Leah had never had before. Joy flowed through every fibre of her body.

That night was the beginning of many more nights of deep intimacy between them. Leah enjoyed listening to him share all the stories he had told before and many more he had left unsaid. He told her how he had wrestled with God, and finally explained why he walked with a limp. Leah laughed at his boldness. "You wrestled with the Almighty God? Jacob, have you no fear?" She teased him and enjoyed the way he embraced her.

She grabbed the bowl besides her and continued to listen to his story; she touched her hands to his lips when he paused to drink from his wine cup, and she fed him dried dates. They prayed together each night and the bond between them deepened by growing stronger each day.

CHAPTER 82

Leah stood behind Jacob as he knelt before his father Isaac. They had finally arrived at Mamre. The joy of the old man was not hidden. He pulled his son to himself in a warm embrace, and they wept on each other's shoulders. They exchanged quiet words between them.

After the reconciliation, Jacob turned around and called her towards his father and introduced her to Isaac. Leah knelt before Isaac and bowed her head to him. The old man was frail, and his sight had failed. He beckoned for her to come closer, and as she drew near to him, he placed his hand on her shoulder. He said, "Beloved of the Lord, chosen by God himself, the mother of kings and kings to come, you are welcome home."

EPILOGUE

*J*acob didn't know when or how it happened, but he woke up one day and realised that Leah's smile made his heart skip a beat. His broken heart had been mended, and he had fallen deeply in love with her. His love for Leah was unexpected and pure; it was tender, and it had grown and matured over the years.

He lay beside her and watched her sleep. Old age had come upon them both, him more than her. Even though her back was turned away from him, he could imagine the curves of her face. Her face was beautiful even in old age. God had been so faithful to them. God had been so patient with him, giving him time to come to this place where he now knew that Leah was a precious gift from God. He remembered all those times when he had prayed to God, angry at Laban's deception, crying out for Rachel, God had always whispered, *"Leah."* This woman, the one who lay in his arms, was the one chosen by God. How was he to know? He should have listened to God instead of his heart and refused to serve Laban anymore; he should have returned home with Leah. But then, he wouldn't have had those wonderful years with Rachel and his beloved Joseph and Benjamin would not have been born. His joy and love came at a great cost; it cost Leah much more than it had cost him. It must have been God who kept her and gave her strength all those years, the years he had been blinded to her existence.

Touching her hair gently, the scent of honey and milk filled his nostrils causing him to draw closer to her to breathe it in. He suddenly felt annoyed that she was fast asleep. He wanted to wake her up; he was desperate to look into her eyes and tell her the truth about how much he has come to love and cherish her in his old age.

Pulling back her hair from her ears, he kissed them gently and whispered, "My Leah, chosen for me by God himself; my heart is filled with deep love and aches for you. Oh, my Leah, how much I love you."

He pulled himself closer into her, his body moulding perfectly behind hers. Jacob laid his head behind hers and drifted into peaceful slumber.

Leah awakened at the sound of Jacob's voice. She listened to him whisper softly into her ears. The words that he had spoken set her heart on fire, and she felt like it would explode with joy. His declaration of love was an unexpected blessing and a wonderful gift. Her soul awakened within her. Choking back the tears that welled up, she closed her eyes and worshipped God.

She knew that He had done this; this was the work of His hands. These last few years with Jacob had been filled with so much joy, and she was grateful for every minute she had with him. She had been grateful to be his left hand and had thought that would be her place forever - always second to her sister. She thought when Rachel died, she would have taken Jacob's heart with her. Maybe that was true in the beginning, but God had restored his heart, for her sake.

Her own ears could not lie to her; she had heard clearly the words Jacob had spoken. She closed her tear-filled eyes and began to pray, "Thank you, God. You have redeemed me this day and given me joy beyond measure. My life is now and forever yours."

Many years later, when Leah died, she was buried by Jacob, in the field of Ephron the Hittite, in the cave in the field at Machpelah, east of Mamre, in the land of Canaan. This is where Jacob instructs his sons to bury him when he dies, to lay him in the burial ground of the Patriarchs right next to Leah, the woman he loves!

AUTHOR'S NOTES

The story of Leah and Rachel is truly fascinating and absorbing. It is one of those stories in the Bible that will leave you with mixed emotions. The first time I read it, although sympathetic to Rachel, my heart went out to Leah. My thoughts were - How did Leah feel? What was life like for her? How did she cope with the rejection? I've tried to imagine myself in her shoes, and each time it leaves me feeling speechless.

It was in my quest to answer these questions that this story was born. I started by pondering, wondering and imagining what it would have been like to have been Leah. I filled the gaps with as much information as I could find and for the rest, I used my imagination.

The message in Leah's story is one that inspires and encourages me. It is amazing to see how God can use a woman who was unwanted and unloved to change history. I feel so strongly in my heart that there are lessons to be learnt and that God truly has something to say, someone to reach, and a truth to teach. He wants to use His word and my creative thoughts as a vehicle to reach His daughters.

Even today, there are *Leahs* amongst us, women who feel

AUTHOR'S NOTES

unnoticed, unwanted, and unloved. Women who need the encouragement found in the pages of this book, and others who I pray will hear from God pertaining to their own unique circumstances.

I do need to state clearly that this book is a work of fiction, based on the truth in the word of God. I did a lot of research to ensure that I could stay close to the truth of the Bible and the history period. This research led me to reading a lot Jewish teachings on this story. I read many books, articles, and watched videos online.

I learnt a lot from Jewish history, some of these details I have incorporated into this story as the Jewish history goes into much more detail about Leah and Rachel than the Bible. For example, they share that Leah and Rachel were identical twins. Both women were beautiful with a similar build.

I also learnt that Leah was betrothed to marry Esau, Jacob's older twin brother. His reputation was poor, and the fear of this union left Leah in continuous mourning and praying to God to change her destiny and this is why she had 'tender eyes'. It was from all the crying.

Jewish history also suggests that their father Laban and the whole community were complicit in the plan to swap brides. Since Jacob's arrival, they had all prospered. They knew he was blessed by God, and this deception was a ploy to keep him longer so they could continue to prosper as a community.

Rachel was opposed to the idea; she had told Jacob all about the wicked plans and between them, they came up with three signs for him to recognise her on their wedding night. However, on the night of the wedding, Rachel took pity on her sister and told her the signs. She wanted to protect her twin sister from the shame of being a rejected bride. This is how they were able to deceive Jacob.

Although this book is a work of fiction, which gives me the creative license to write it freely, I made the decision to choose

AUTHOR'S NOTES

the Bible as the main point of reference for this book. It is what I know and believe to be true and so I used all the information in the Bible and my imagination filled in the remainder.

I have, however, borrowed some information from Jewish history. The parts of this story that I know to be true are found in the book of Genesis. I'd encourage you to read it for yourself as I believe it is important to separate the fact from fiction.

I have used information from various parts of the book of Genesis, drawing some details of Jacob's earlier life before he came to live with his uncle. I hope that after reading this book, it will give you a real desire to dig deep into the word of God and fall in love with it all over again.

It has taken me over three years to write this book. I'd like to say it was because of deep historical research and prayer, but the truth is it was simply fear. That's the real reason. I just strongly believed the lie that I didn't have what it takes to write a novel and so I settled in the nonfiction zone, convincing myself to focus on truth and not made-up stories. Still, I felt unfulfilled as an author.

I struggled with the burning desire to pour out my creativity through fiction. I know that in my own personal life, I have learnt a lot from non-fiction as well as fiction. Why else would God have given me this incredible gift if it wasn't for me to use? How can a blessing feel like a curse? Words unexpressed choking the life out of my very soul, I felt empty and dry.

God has blessed me with a creative mind. I use it to entertain myself most days and many times I find myself so drawn into my imaginary world that I become short tempered with those in my real world for disturbing my thoughts. Hilarious I know and somewhat disturbing.

I share this to say, for me, my creative mind is real and precious and the fear of putting it in words, words that can be shared with the world makes me feel anxious and somewhat

AUTHOR'S NOTES

exposed, and the very persistent question beckons "what if they don't like it?" Or worse, "What if I don't do it justice?"

"What if I'm the only one who enjoys it?"

What if, what if, what if…

I've had to come to a place with God where I choose to walk in obedience – obedience over fear, to simply try and tell the story, trusting that He will guide my mind, heart, and words. He is a God of creation, the God of creativity. The one who has gifted me, created me, and is my best bud (and SAVIOUR), Jesus, is a master storyteller himself, so I'm in safe hands. I just have to trust and obey.

I personally invite you into the world of *LEAH*. Whilst Rachel was Jacob's desire, Leah, was God's design.

ABOUT THE AUTHOR

Amanda Bedzrah is married to Francois and they have three wonderful children. They live in the county of Kent, best known as "The Garden of England" in the United Kingdom. Amanda is the founder of Empower a Woman, a UK based non-profit organisation set up to meet the needs of vulnerable women and children.

Amanda is a passionate Bible teacher, an inspirational speaker, a prayer minister, and a senior NHS professional. She is a Law graduate (LLB Hons), she is also certified in Business Analysis Practice and Project Management.

Find out more

ALSO BY AMANDA BEDZRAH

Praying Proverbs
5 Habits of Godly Resilient Women
The Love That Set Me Free
Overcoming the Fear of Death